About the Author

T.S. Marni is a pseudonym for three sisters who grew up in Hong Kong, where they lived for some years in Buxey Lodge. They frequently popped into the Beaconsfield post office and travelled past The Hermitage on their way to The Island School. They have lived in India, the U.K. and the U.S. The Marnis hatched the plot for *Blood, With A Drop of Sherry* while on a holiday, during which they 'endured' the hilarious antics of a particularly pompous guest.

Background of Buxey Lodge and Chater Hall

From Buxey Lodge the Marni sisters often visited friends at
Chater Hall – both buildings are identical, situated at either ends
of the famous Conduit Road in Hong Kong.
The land that the buildings are on were originally owned,
in the early 1900s, by Sir Hormusjee Mody and Sir Paul Chater.
Buxey Lodge is named after Sir Mody's uncle and benefactor,
Jehangirjee Buxey. Sir Mody and Sir Chater were a remarkable
team and men of great vision. They formed the company
'Chater & Mody' in 1868 and went on to be pioneers in the
early development of Hong Kong, developing the stock
exchange, the bullion market, the port, land reclamation and
financing numerous institutions that shape the vibrant city that
Hong Kong became.

Blood, With A Drop of Sherry

T.S. Marni

Blood, With a Drop of Sherry

Olympia Publishers
London

www.olympiapublishers.com
OLYMPIA PAPERBACK EDITION

First Published in 2024

Olympia Publishers
Tallis House
2 Tallis Street
London
EC4Y 0AB

Printed in Great Britain

Dedication

For Mum and Dad, who made Buxey Lodge our cosy haven and our life in Hong Kong magical.

Contents

The Homecoming 11

Let the Party Begin 17

And the Party Ends! 28

Above One's Station in Life 36

Tears, Cheese and News 43

A Funeral That Happened 51

The Dawn 57

Sherry's Chance 62

From the Same Pot 70

Lady Fussington and the Screwallahs 75

It's a Case Of 'Either/Or' 83

Aspirations 89

A, B, C & D 96

Francis, Phyllis and Mary 102

A Picture Paints a Thousand Words 114

… From Gypsies to the Great and the Good…................119

Suppositions..122

Realisations 129

Nothing in Life Is Black and White...............136

Plans...142

A.R. and S.R. 145

Interview Aftermath.....................................154

Possession Lane 159

The S.P. and Bartholomew 166

Glenealy House...171

The Police and the Suspects............................177

From Buxey Lodge to Willowbund Police Station........183

The Bloomin' Bloom 189

The Monsoon 192

From Willowbund to Buxey 196

The Clouds, the Fog and the Rain...................201

From Twilight to Dawn...................................205

Forty-Eight Hours After the Accident 208

The Set-up...213

Explanations and Exclamations 218

Chapter One

The Homecoming

The bright red Audi Cabriolet sped along proudly, before finally beginning its long, tedious ascent up the famous and somewhat treacherous Ghat road leading through the Western Ghats of south India up to The Nilgiris district and to its final destination, the historical hill station town of Ooty.

Effortlessly weaving through the weekend traffic, AJ decided that to navigate this very steep road, with its sheer drops and few, if any, guardrails, one had to be either a very experienced driver, as he was, or an absolute lunatic! As he sped upwards, he threw the occasional glance to his right, soaking in the spectacular view of the endless plains.

He grimaced as he imagined what it must have been like, making one's way on horseback when this road must have been nothing but a rudimentary bridle path, hundreds of years ago. He shuddered at the thought. Yes, AJ Panniker definitely did not possess the sturdy genes of the empire builders! Little did he know that his home state housed the highest number of India's extraordinary Ghat roads, each of which was an engineering feat of the British Raj, so eager had they been to rush up these mountains to escape the deadly heat and disease of the infamous Indian summer.

Thanking his lucky stars that he was a twenty-first century man, he grinned as he threw his Beckham shades onto the white leather passenger seat. How pleased he was to have brought this gem over to India with him. The hefty transportation costs, not to mention the staggering import duty, were well worth it. This gorgeous car would, for sure, help his grand entrance into Nilgiris high society.

The Nilgiris has been called, rather glibly, the Scotland of India. Notwithstanding the uncanny similarity to much of typical British riding country, there are myriad reasons why many of India's upper crust choose to call this part of the country their home. It is an exciting, intriguing, and unique corner of the world.

Recalling well the curves and twists of this road, he changed gears, knowing that the hairpin bends would soon wind, like steel wire coils, tightening their grip on weary travellers. Hopefully, it wouldn't be too bad this time. As a child he never liked travelling back up to the hills after their holidays, even though it meant an escape from the hot, dusty plains. It was car sickness that worried him. All those sick bags his mother used to store in their Ambassador car. It was horribly unpleasant to be throwing up like that. What his stupid mother never understood, was that if you're car sick, you still feel dreadfully ill long after the drive is over!

Yes, how he dreaded those trips back home.

The dusty, hot climate of the plains gradually transformed into cooler, fresher air. The road stretched onwards, the car taking each sharp turn in its stride. The scenery now took on a calm, serene quality. Lush green vegetation began to emerge from all sides. The air now carried a definite scent, one of crushed cypress leaves with a faint whiff of eucalyptus.

To AJ, the dramatic change in scenery from what it was a mere hour ago was a welcome relief from the long tiring journey from England. Come to think of it, he mused, the town he once called home, did remind him of the home he had now left behind, more precisely, the Surrey hills. Pangs of sadness tugged at his heart... and dare he admit, a touch of... remorse? ... He thought of his luxurious two storey home with its perfectly landscaped garden, now sold and forever left behind.

Was all that hard work a wasted effort? Perhaps not. After all, he had made a considerable profit from its sale; and what timing too, selling it right before the property market started to turn.

Always having a knack for spotting the best time and opportunity to make money, AJ was, in the opinion of anyone who knew him, one of the lucky ones. He was confident that this was going to be the type of homecoming he had been dreaming of, thanks to his brilliant idea for the development of his property in Ooty. A genius plan which had begun to take shape in his mind months earlier. AJ was determined that this development was going to be unparalleled, even awesome! And to think of the gossip! Yes... with immense satisfaction, he pictured the 'oohing and aahing' from those he would soon be reacquainted with.

Had it really been eighteen years since he was last in India? How he had managed to stay away for that amount of time was anyone's guess, but in his heart, he knew it was because of their minuscule minds. That was the real reason. Small town mentality creates insular thinkers!

A battered but sturdy lorry suddenly appeared from nowhere, speeding downhill. It was one of the numerous agricultural vehicles making daily trips up and down to the plains. Precariously overloaded with freshly harvested carrots and cabbages, it braked alarmingly close to the Audi. Being the experienced driver that he was, AJ quickly squeezed as far as he could to the left, avoiding it by a hair's breadth.

As his wheels continued up the steep road, random, fleeting memories swept through AJ's mind. He wondered what Francis was doing these days, where all of his other friends were and what they were up to? Actually, come to think of it, they had never really been his friends. Just a bunch of silly small-town people, who knew nothing of the outside world. No sophistication. They had never experienced the world as he had, what on earth could they know of life outside their little bubble? Yes, he was indeed looking forward to giving them all a good shake up with his grand plans.

Ooty, of course, held many other memories for AJ. It was where he was born, grew up and went to school. Thinking of school, he blinked automatically, as if he was once again on the cross-country route. It seemed as if the blinding sun was, once again, blurring his vision as he ran across the downs under the endless blue sky. He remembered how he would run past the Toda villages, with their strange short houses with domed roofs and women with long ringlets sitting in groups, all draped in those red embroidered shawls. He had always thought that these Toda villages looked quite incongruous, as if they had just popped out of a painting and without rhyme or reason – plonk! – landed on the ground. Even the Todas, rather aptly, had no idea where they came from; all they knew was that they came from an unknown land, with their buffaloes, to these pristine pastures.

Ooty, or Ootacamund, to use the full version of its name, is where he learned to fend for himself because his parents most certainly never did anything for him, apart from storing the sick bags in that horrid family car. Being an only child, he never had siblings to fall back on for support and company in the way that Francis did. How jealous and sad he used to feel, hearing about his friends over the years happily enjoying life. Faces from the past popped up in his head. Yuck! A dismal lot if there ever was one! It was because of these people that AJ was determined to make something of himself. His presence must be felt this time around, and yup, he knew now for sure, he would never have to look back!

He suddenly switched his attention to himself. The twelve or so hairpin bends he had so expertly manoeuvred were now taking their toll, and AJ was beginning to feel that familiar twinge rising in his stomach. It was just coming up to noon. Another one and a half hours before he would arrive at the Ootacamund Country Club, or rather his club because that would soon be his too. Smirking, and determined to disregard his nauseousness, he decided to plan the next few days. An exclusive soiree had to be planned, with, as the saying goes, no expense spared. It was definitely his number one priority. AJ needed everyone to see him and know that he had arrived. After which he wanted to carry out a full inspection of the Chater Hall property, which, if all went according to plan, held the promise of a huge development, not to mention the prosperity it would bring to the town... all the jobs that he, the magnanimous AJ Panniker, would be creating. In fact, it occurred to him on a number of occasions, that he might have to think seriously about running for the Indian parliament. After all, what was the point of doing all these noble deeds if it didn't follow that he would walk amongst the great and the good. The more his mind worked over his plans for the next few weeks, the more he realised there was simply no time to waste.

Without warning, a packed bus, with a sea of faces hanging out of the windows staring down at him like a circus house of horrors, hammered past, blaring its horn at his car. 'Hah! Clearly jealous of my car,' was his last thought before screeching to a halt. Tumbling out, he grabbed his impossibly expensive Armani scarf and covered his face. He simply could not bear to be identified, especially not here, and certainly not under these circumstances. Lurching forward, he began to violently vomit.

Chapter Two

Let the Party Begin

Facing the mirror, he adjusted his collar. How pleased he was with the reflection before him. "Hmmmm... think about all the gorgeous women soon to be falling at your feet," the stocky man muttered to himself, as pudgy fingers ran through his thinning hair. There was no mistaking that AJ was indeed extremely well turned out this morning. As much as could be done to revamp and upgrade the existing exterior, had been done. Pale pink linen shirt, indigo chinos, and navy suede Belgian loafers gave the finishing touches to what, he undoubtedly assumed, would be his successful entrée into Nilgiri society. Clearly, there was not much which could be improved upon!

So far, the weather looked clear. Provided there was nothing more than a light drizzle, the shoes should be fine. For him, today's garden party was simply a matter of putting a perfect foot forward before being embraced by his future admirers.

AJ left his spare shoes with the receptionist, asking her to make sure she kept a close eye on them as they were very pricey. The receptionist smiled and nodded, although as soon as he had turned away her easy smile disappeared into pursed lips. AJ had not endeared himself with the staff since his arrival a few days ago. Ali Rasheed, the club secretary, stood some distance from the reception area. He had tucked himself discreetly away in a corner, giving himself a good view of the comings and goings of his guests. He made a mental note to keep his eye on this one.

As AJ stood on the gleaming wooden floor of the lobby, his thoughts went back to his arrival at the club. Smiling to himself, he remembered the startled look on the receptionist's face when she looked up to see him standing in front of her. Quite a nice change from the usual type of guest she had to deal with, he hazarded. After a swift glance around the impressive yet understated lobby, AJ's summation of 'Typical Club Types' was firmly confirmed. Members seated in the lounge, members enjoying pre-lunch drinks at the bar, and members who were simply milling about, had, every single one of them, reinforced his opinion on the subject. Drab. Unimpressive. Dull. He smirked as he realised that the acronym for his description was D U D! Yes, they even looked like duds!

Preoccupied with his amusing thoughts, and totally oblivious of the piercing looks from Ali, he turned to peer through the arched windows at the perfectly manicured grass on the Camellia Lawn, where guests had begun to arrive for the annual garden party, officially called 'The President's Tea'.

He recalled childhood chit chat about the club's annual garden party, his parents talking about the fancy-pancy invitees and even what outfits may be on display. The President's Tea was, and is to this day, held at the height of the summer season, when the club rooms are all occupied.

He knew that invitations were sent out, well in advance, to the crème de la crème of Nilgiri society. Members staying at the club were invited, all the members of the club committee were present and, of course, the host, the club president, presided over it all.

AJ's mother, Saras, had been an accomplished seamstress as well as being a talented embroiderer. Saras Panniker was an Ooty girl, who, sadly, was orphaned when she was just eleven. Although she had a kindly aunt, her mother's sister, Saranya, the aunt's husband never let her take on the child, and so she was placed in the St. Alicia Convent, located on the outskirts of the town. Thankfully, Saras had a good, grounded childhood as the nuns were kind and nurturing and, to top it off, she had her loving aunt, who never failed to visit every week during her seven years in the convent. It was the mission of the nuns of the St. Alicia Convent to teach their female wards dressmaking, and more importantly, their true passion, hand embroidery. When the young Saras left the convent at eighteen, she was able to set up a small business of her own where she took on commissions from the locals. And so it came about that, through her business, she was privy to all the gossip about who was attending this most magnificent of all summertime soirées.

AJ threw a rare thought up to his mother in heaven, well, the tables are well and truly turned now! Never in her wildest dreams would Mama have imagined that I would be a showstopper at this posh event. It was now time to make a grand entrance. Allowing himself a quick once-over in the lobby mirror and pleased with what he saw, AJ stepped out into the sun.

So, here he was, at the 112th gathering of the annual President's Tea, the Ootacamund Country Club's ultimate answer to get visiting summer members to meet the elite of The Nilgiris and, of course, the illustrious members of the club committee.

The Camellia Lawn, aptly named for its white and pink camellia bushes, was filling up alarmingly quickly. Alarmingly for the club staff that is, and, with their comedic scurrying around, it was plain to see that they were certainly not coping very well.

In keeping with the dress code, ladies resplendent in brilliantly hued silk saris, floral print shifts and fashionable dresses, stepped out with their smartly dressed 'other halves', many clutching umbrellas in case the weather took a turn for the worse.

Surveying the scene as keenly as a birdwatcher would, AJ looked for familiar faces and as he did so, his beady eyes caught one particular figure. Memories flooded back, him in his red shorts, holding his mother's hand as she chatted away to Mrs. Mary Mendoza. He was astounded at how well she looked. She seemed barely a few years older than she did twenty years ago. He made a note to catch up with her later on.

There were far more people than he had expected. Maybe they had diluted the invitation list and added people from the trades, he thought uncharitably. But he quickly changed his mind, for his experienced eye noted true blue-blooded socialites, new money and old. High society opulence and modern-day chic collided in spectacular style. Dressed to the nines, they all looked frightfully distinguished, not to mention wealthy.

Parties were actually a nightmare for AJ; there was always an element of chaos and surprise at these large gatherings. One just never knew who you would bump into. You could run into an old enemy, an old friend, an old friend who's become an enemy... It was a gamble and that's why he found them so stressful. Never mind, he sighed to himself. With his plans for Chater Hall, they would all be lining up for the pickings!

Taking a deep breath, he plunged into the vast sea of the blue blooded; picking up a glass of Scotch from a passing waiter, he made a beeline for the ultimate prize of them all.

Ali's sharp eyes followed him closely. Recalling their brief conversation at the Queen's Bar the evening before, the resentment he had felt at the time came flooding back. He was absolutely appalled at the man's buffoonery.

Just think of it, an overseas Indian returning after all these years away and thinking he could barge in and buy up the club! This magnificent historical institution was going to be converted into a luxury spa. The very thought of such a deed was enough to bring tears to his eyes. "Well, over my dead body, sir... or perhaps yours," he said to himself as he continued watching AJ closely. However, his irritation quickly turned to alarm as he realised that AJ was now having what looked like a very serious conversation with none other than the club president himself, Brigadier Johnny Chacko.

His heart sank. He could see the Brigadier was all ears. He had no idea of what it was that AJ was holding forth about but suspected that he was lobbying for the Brig. to start the ball rolling on his ridiculous idea to buy the club. It wasn't possible, in any case. People can't just buy up clubs, all clubs are owned by their members, he thought. Unless, of course, there's some loophole I don't know about. Before he could get even more anxious, he noticed that Mary had interrupted the two men. Armed with her inimitable charm, she gave them each a peck and started twittering. Despite the distance, Ali Rasheed could see AJ was disappointed that his monologue had been abruptly cut short. He also realised, with great glee, that getting the ear of the Brigadier once again, was not going to be easy as the Brigadier was off on a trip to New Delhi any day now. Not surprisingly, AJ drifted off. Mary and Johnny were now having a very lively chat and the sun was once again shining for poor Ali Rasheed.

"My, my. So, it is you! I heard from the rumour mill that you were back, but honestly, I had to see you in the flesh to believe it. So, back after all this time, eh?"

That was a very familiar voice returning from the distant past. AJ swung around to face an attractive woman who must have been in her mid-forties. For a fleeting instant he could not recall where he knew her from, but a moment later, the penny dropped. She was none other than Pearl. Pearl Veeraswamy, he realised with unhappiness. He had dated her sister. An unfortunate, messy story, a lifetime ago. It felt strange seeing her after such a long time. In many ways, she looked so much like Avril.

Attractive though she was, her age was clearly starting to show. He observed her face closely while deliberating a witty comeback. Little crows' feet etched around the corners of her eyes and small wrinkles covered a face that had once been pretty. He supposed this was to be expected. Life and all its happenings do take their toll on all of us eventually, he mused. He wondered how she had fared and what she had done with her life since her sister's death.

"Yes, Pearl, back because I have missed home so much! It's amazing seeing all my good friends after all these years. What a long time it's been. How are you?" Despite his uncertainty and a tummy filled with butterflies, he sallied forth with a wide grin, trying hard to push away the sad memories of Avril.

His attempt to greet Pearl with a peck on the cheek was rejected and, much to his embarrassment, he could sense people around him had noticed the awkward exchange. "You were gone for so long, AJ. We rather thought we would never, ever see you again. When I heard you'd returned, I absolutely did not believe it. I mean, this is so… so… so out of the blue. After all these years. Anyway, what are you doing here? You can't have really missed us or this town. Up to your usual no good, perhaps?" she asked with an arched brow.

He most certainly didn't like where this conversation was leading, not in the least and, more worryingly, he noticed more familiar faces walking in his general direction. God, he thought, a downmarket moment if there ever was one! But just at that moment, and saving his bacon, the music began.

A live band began playing one of his all-time old favourites, Blondie's 'Heart of Glass'.

"Heck, the music's very loud. Shall we move to the other end?" AJ had found his escape. Moving to a quieter spot on the lawn, Pearl said, "AJ, let me reintroduce you to my dear friends, Phyllis and Geoffrey."

A stunning woman appeared on the scene, hand in hand with a man chewing on a cigar. They looked quite the couple. Phyllis hugged Pearl warmly and Geoffrey gave her a kiss. Phyllis was dressed to kill. Every man at the party was staring at her, not least because of her plunging neckline. It left little to the imagination. She exuded poise and confidence. Ali, however, was watching her with great disapproval; he wondered what had happened to the elegant graciousness of all those lady members in the not so recent past. Ali thought, 'What on earth is happening to people nowadays? They are either downright rude, or else they dress atrociously.' But that was Ali Rasheed, most of the other men were discreetly enjoying the view.

"Are you the man everyone's been talking about?" It sounded more like a challenge than a question.

AJ had been rather taken aback by the sight of Phyllis; mesmerised by her was probably more accurate. He hauled himself back to the present.

"Uhm, yes, I guess I must be the man," he said. "And you are?"

"Geoffrey Payton, old boy!" he bellowed. AJ almost expected a heavy thump on his back as Geoffrey continued, "So, you were an Ooty boy at one time and then fled to Queen and Country, eh? Well, welcome back. Are you planning on staying long?"

Geoffrey laughed loudly as he and AJ shook hands.

AJ had never met Geoffrey before as he had arrived in The Nilgiris long after AJ decided to make his fortune in England. An Englishman might prove very useful in drumming up business for the Chater project. A former Londoner, Geoffrey had made Ooty his home over fifteen years ago. He was an architect who had made a name for himself with his eco-friendly designs for an array of buildings ranging from luxury resorts and office buildings to opulent homes.

"Good to meet you, Geoffrey. In actual fact, I've come back for good. My property investments here have done pretty well but not as well as they might have done. I'm afraid the long distance has made it difficult to manage from the Surrey hills; you do know the Surrey hills, of course. Impossible to trust some of the rogues out here. And you say you're an architect? I'm in the building business, too, so let's meet up soon for a chat, eh? So, yes, here I am, back in good old Ooty and loving it even though it's only been a couple of days. I'd love to sit down with you and tell you my plans to resurrect Ooty. Drag it into the twenty-first century. I'm dedicating my property, Chater Hall, to the common people. I mean, hand it over to them by creating the best and only shopping mall in the town. Can you imagine the jobs that will be created and the opportunities for businesses? Anyway, before I get into the details, who might this be?" he asked as he grinned sideways at Phyllis.

Phyllis ignored him and continued her avid conversation with Pearl. She refused to look at AJ, despite Geoffrey's attempts to coax her into the conversation.

The sounds of jollity added a sparkling, frenetic energy to what was turning out to be a very lively party. AJ was beginning to think it was time to move on. There were so many people to get reacquainted with. In the distance, he could see a lady trying unsuccessfully to control her fat dogs. He vaguely remembered her.

"Did I hear the name Chater Hall?" It was Phyllis who had started talking, as the very mention of Chater Hall had piqued her interest, but before he could open his mouth, something happened to AJ.

In a moment that could only be described as surreal, he felt himself being violently thrust forward, falling face down onto a bed of flowers with a great big thud.

He opened his eyes and spat out a mouthful of soil, part of his shirt sleeve was torn, and had wet soil sand stuck all over it. Raising his head, he saw what had happened. Those bloody dogs had jumped on him from behind, and the damn things were still bounding around him, preventing him from making an urgent escape from this God-awful situation.

The dogs' owner grabbed back the leashes of her Golden Retrievers, Honey and Misty, and apologised profusely to AJ. Geoffrey was quick to help him up, adding further embarrassment. AJ scowled at the dogs. He hated dogs, ever since he was bitten by one as a child. Nursing a sore elbow, he was suddenly confronted by a sea of familiar faces.

Finally, it dawned on him that Phyllis was none other than Phyllis Fonseca, and was that her brother, Francis, in the distance, both of whom he used to play with all those years ago? Her family had once owned Chater Hall, until his father made a smart business decision to buy the house and at the same time, in his charitable way, save Phyllis's family from financial ruin. All things considered, she could have at least shown him the courtesy of acknowledging him. After all, her family owed him. Then there was the dog lady, for God's sake, he knew her too! He realised she was Anna Screwallah. She was just standing there, stupidly staring at him. It now came back to him that the Screwallahs lived somewhere near Chater Hall. All these sudden realisations made his head hurt. Was it the fall, he wondered? Can knocks on one's head bring back long-lost memories?

"Not hurt, are we, AJ? And what was that you were saying about Chater Hall?" sneered Phyllis.

A sea of eyes stared back at him, some in shock, some amused, and some with malice…

Chapter Three

And the Party Ends!

It was a cool, misty night with a steady drizzle coming down since the late afternoon, in stark contrast to the bright weather enjoyed at the garden party earlier that day. In fact, it never drizzled at this time of the year, summer. One either had a heavy afternoon shower that cleansed the air, or the day remained beautifully sunny. But as always, you could never say 'never'.

Fortunately, for members of the Ootacamund Country Club, the clubhouse was warm and cosy and filled with the happy buzz of being busy, busy, busy. All the guest rooms were occupied and anyone wishing to stay would now have to wait weeks before a room became available.

Earlier in the evening, the fireplace at the popular Queen's Bar had been lit, giving out a welcoming glow and drawing people inside. The club was a popular haunt, not only for the guests staying at the club, but also for the many well-to-do, affluent members who made Ooty, and the neighbouring town of Coonoor, their home. The crux of the matter was that Ooty had not been blessed with a good choice of such venues. Those that did exist simply could not live up to the high standards of the club. The service and food were beyond reproach, not to mention its elegant, old-world ambience, which was a major attraction. It transported patrons back to a bygone era. Stepping through its doors and on to gleamingly polished Burma teak floors, one was greeted by a faint whiff of wood polish mixed with candle wax and Silvo. The walls were mounted with trophies glorifying the hunting days of the Great Raj, and massive, vibrant oil paintings depicting scenes from seventeenth and eighteenth-century India, giving the club a surprising lift of colour. History had soaked well into the walls of this institution, giving it the character that so many had loved through generations.

It was getting late. At well past midnight, guests were beginning to retire to their rooms. Local members began making their way to the main entrance to call their drivers, who would whisk them safely home.

Yet, there were always the usual barflies who preferred to linger, hoping the evening would never end. Without exception, those at the club this evening had attended the garden party that day. As the afternoon drifted to early evening, groups of friends simply did not have the heart to disband.

Chief amongst them was Geoffrey, who had lived in India for several years when he was young, as his parents were missionaries in India. When he turned eleven, they sent him back to boarding school in England. He hated that he had been separated from his parents and hated it even more that he had to leave his friends in India. It also did not help that he had become rather attached to the way of life in the country of his birth. These disappointments had made him determined to make the most of boarding school life in

England, which for him meant making as much mischief as possible!

Putting his arm around Phyllis's waist, his partner of just a few months, Geoffrey laughed out loud. It was the sort of laugh that invariably captured the attention of anyone in his vicinity. His friends looked up in anticipation of being entertained with yet another hilarious story.

"Oh, my goodness, Geoffrey, you have got to be joking. How did you manage to smuggle so many cigarette packets into the dorm?"

Phyllis's raucous laughter competed fiercely with Geoffrey's. She was a well-known personality in Ooty, not least for the fact that she was the fourth generation of a well-loved local family. Phyllis always lived life to its fullest. She decided early on in her life that she would not be tied down to a husband and children. Those were responsibilities she could well do without. There were a few niggling worries, such as where she would live when she retired, an event that was not in the too distant future; yet she preferred to throw caution to the wind. So here she was, at one of her favourite haunts, sharing good stories with her friends, Ben and Usha Menon, and her childhood friend, Pearl.

It was the here-and-now that mattered, not tomorrow, yesterday, or yesteryear. Her sister, Violet, and her husband, Arun, had just left, after having reluctantly agreed to stay for yet another 'last drink'. How washed out and nervy Violet was looking, thought Phyllis as she hugged them a hurried goodbye.

Lighting yet another cigarette, Ben inhaled deeply and looked at Phyllis. "You do know, don't you, that our friend

Geoffrey here was the school rowing champion before he was unceremoniously suspended for the rest of the rowing season for letting the headmaster's Rhodesian Ridgebacks out?"

Usha started giggling, "Honestly, Geoffrey, why would you do such a thing and get into trouble at such an important time?"

"Quite right I was, and proud of myself, too. I was the only kid who had the guts to let those poor cooped-up dogs out for a good run across the fields. Of course, having been hemmed in, in that titchy garden, once they were out, they weren't in any hurry to come back home." He laughed out loudly again. "Remember that song when we were in school, 'Who Let the Dogs Out?' That song was popular at the same time, and I was really tempted to play it loudly every time we walked past his gates!"

Phyllis glanced at the antique clock sitting at the end of the bar table and then looked straight at Geoffrey with a glint in her green eyes. "Oh, darling Geoffrey, it's getting so late, and I have to be up on time tomorrow. Can we get home, do you think?"

"Yes, best we get going; I have a meeting with the Sri Lankans early tomorrow morning…"

Pulling her shawl around her arms, Usha said, "Pearl darling, we can drop you back." She smiled kindly at Pearl, knowing the poor girl was rather rattled earlier at the garden party, although she didn't know why. She must get all the details later from someone who would be in-the-know!

At just this moment, a shrill shriek rang through the club. It pierced the air, startling everyone in the room. The heavy crystal glass that Geoffrey had been taking good care of only a moment ago, smashed onto the floor, sending shattered shards of glass upwards onto Phyllis's dress.

Shocked, she screamed. Geoffrey and Pearl quickly helped pick the glass bits off her clothes. The atmosphere in the room was one of chaotic excitement with an eagerness to know the 'what and why', mixed with nervous thoughts of what might or might not now unfold...

The bartenders rushed into the hallway to find out what on earth had happened, but they only managed an ungainly collision with a terror-stricken waiter scurrying towards them, the source of the unseemly racket. Terribly dishevelled and bawling away, he brushed them aside and rushed into the Queen's Bar, still screaming, and frantically waving his arms in the air in no particular direction.

"He's dead! Oh, God, he's dead. Help! Help! Get a doctor! No! Not a doctor! He's already dead! Help! HELP ME, get someone." Looking wild-eyed, clearly in shock, and having reverted to his own language of Tamil, the hysterical waiter quickly descended into incoherency.

Geoffrey, who generally liked to feel in control of any situation thrown at him, decided to take charge of the situation quickly. Grabbing the distraught waiter by the shoulders, he gave him a vigorous shake, telling him to pull himself together.

"Come on, boy! Explain yourself, slowly and clearly. It's no use shouting orders at us. It's us who should be telling you what to do. Now out with it!" Luckily for 'the boy', almost all those in the room understood Tamil very well.

Geoffrey's actions seemed to have the desired effect. As they all crowded around him, snippets of information emerged erratically. He had gone to a guest's room to clear the dinner trolley and found the man dead... he thinks he's dead... "But he can't be dead... he playing biiiig joke on us," wailed the waiter.

He suddenly stopped and stood silently staring, boggle eyed, at his audience. He was obviously in shock.

Silence fell on the room as his audience drank in his astonishing and confusing proclamations. Their numb thoughts were broken a few seconds later by the club manager, who had rushed in. He had heard the shrieking despite the long corridors.

Standing at the doorway, Ali Rasheed decided that whatever the situation was, he had to act quickly. He could vaguely hear doors opening and closing in other parts of the club. Obviously, guests were alarmed. They may all turn up at the bar, perhaps even in their pyjamas... how unbecoming! The last thing he wanted was gossip, especially during this important tourist season. He had to do his level best to contain matters.

Pulling himself up a few inches, he announced rather grandly, albeit with much self-doubt, "We have an incident here so I must ask all of you who are not staying at the club to kindly leave. Thank you for your cooperation. Those who are staying here, please make yourselves comfortable in the bar. You will be served drinks on the house. Please be patient as we find out what exactly has happened. I assure you there is nothing to worry about."

He swiftly took off with the hysterical waiter and one of the barmen, leaving the other to make sure his orders were followed.

Poor Phyllis was still picking out bits of glass from her clothes. Geoffrey stared at the retreating staff; he looked lost, very much wondering why he hadn't been asked to tag along.

Making their way through the corridors, the three men turned right and walked down a beautifully lit rosewood-panelled passage. The framed photographs of old Ooty town and countryside scenes stared back at them as they picked up the pace. Further down, towards the end of the corridor, Ali could see that the door to room number four was wide open. With his heart thumping loudly, he slowly approached the room. All was quiet... eerily so. He could sense the fear and trepidation emanating from the waiter who was following closely behind him and clutching the corner of his jacket, much as a fearful child would do.

Peering inside, he could see two of the club's famous bread rolls lying on the carpet along with an upturned silver butter dish, no doubt ruining the pale Kashmiri carpet with its grease. The wine glass was on the carpet, the red wine had soaked straight through it. The valuable carpet would have to go, he thought, sighing to himself.

Then, what he saw made his heart almost miss a beat, or maybe it did miss a beat.

The body of a man, facing them, sitting at the dining table, was slumped forward, his face submerged in a large bowl of soup. The sight was grotesque. Had he drowned in the soup?

"I just don't believe this! He must have had a heart attack or stroke, or a fit of some kind."

Looking at him, quite dead, he felt a weight lift from his chest. A strange feeling of relief engulfed him but before he could enjoy this new sensation he was interrupted by a sudden cry from behind. He turned to see Phyllis rushing in with Geoffrey close behind her, panting away and hot on her heels.

"AJ Panniker! What on earth!" cried Phyllis. No one was laughing now.

Chapter Four

Above One's Station in Life

Hearing Tiffany's friendly bark, Sherry Darling realised that her guest would be arriving any moment now. Never ceasing to be amazed at the incredible intuition of animals, she counted the exact seconds as to when she would hear the doorbell ring.

She did a quick check of her hair and adjusted her coral beads in front of the oval hall mirror before opening the door with a wide smile.

"Good morning! So gorgeous to see you, my dear!"

This was her trademark welcome for all her friends, and Mary Mendoza was one of her closest. Hugs and kisses were warmly exchanged. Sherry got the familiar whiff of Mary's signature perfume, the rich deep fragrance of Madame Rochas.

Sherry had barely opened her eyes that morning when she received a call from Mary insisting on visiting her as she had something important to tell her. Hearing the soft urgency in her voice, Sherry's curiosity was piqued.

After giving instructions to the maid, Philomena, she spent a good half hour wondering which crockery set to use for the occasion, before deciding on the yellow cuckoo set. Perfection was everything to Sherry.

There was still enough time for a walk in the garden with Tiffany before Mary arrived. Looking at the view across the valley, she smiled, recalling the time when Zareen first interviewed Philomena. What a silly argument they had about her name! With Zareen insisting it was 'Ploomina'!

The problem was that the Tamil language simply does not have a phonetic pronunciation for the syllables 'eff' and 'fer'. So, when a Tamil-speaking person has to say a word with these sounds, one would invariably get a 'pler' or 'ploo' and this is why Philomena pronounced her name 'Ploomina' at her interview and was why Zareen thought that was her name. Honestly, such confusion despite the fact that the Tamil language only happens to be the oldest living language in the world… of course, not that that had anything to do with this problem, she concluded sagely.

It was now time to bring her attention back to the present and her soon-to-be-arriving guest. Strolling back to the house, she eyed the black-eyed Susans with their delicate tendrils climbing up and clinging to the posts of the porch. She loved these happy flowers. Entering, she was greeted with the inviting aroma of baking cake wafting through the house.

If there was one thing Sherry loved to do more than anything, it was to entertain friends in the lovely home which she shared with her cousin, Zareen.

Zareen was half Parsi and half Anglo-Indian. She was a nurse, although she only took on commissions of home nursing to the rich. This was not because Zareen was in any way snobby, but because she realised a long time ago that she had the manners and breeding required in such homes. It was near impossible for these families or individuals to get someone of Zareen's background, so, naturally, she was very highly paid.

The name of their home was Buxey Lodge. Buxey, as they called it, was an old but large, bright, and sturdy construction. Built in 1876 and adhering to the sprawling style of that time, Buxey was indeed a luxury the two ladies could have ill-afforded with their own means. Zareen had inherited it from an uncle on the Parsi side of her family and she had it rented out for the years she was working away from Ooty.

As her permanent move back to The Nilgiris coincided with Sherry's early retirement, they decided to move into the house together. Buxey was set on a hillock and looked down and across a tea estate. It was a wonderful location and the view of the seamless, refreshing green of the tea was constant right through the year.

Sherry had only recently retired from her position at The Wardrop School, the most prestigious secondary school in south India, and when it came down to it, probably in the entire country. Many of India's rich and famous, the movers and shakers, politicians and Bollywood personalities, had been schooled there. She was extremely proud to have worked at WARDS, as it was affectionately called, and felt she had made a real contribution to society through her work. But having worked there for well over twenty-seven years, she decided that when the principal, Alan Cook, retired, it was finally, and sadly, time to call it a day.

Considering all the years she had worked loyally for Principal Cook, she just could not contemplate getting used to someone new, who, in any case, had an enormous ego, from what she had heard. The thought made her shudder. Leaving her job also meant leaving the comfortable accommodation the school had provided; luckily for her, though, her resignation coincided with Zareen's return from Bangalore.

What Sherry loved best about her cousin was her easy-going, laid-back personality. It didn't matter to Zareen in the slightest if Sherry stamped her own mark on Buxey, and so Sherry, known for her quick thinking and organisational abilities, did just that. Yes, Sherry had earned well, saved well, and had always lived well.

Now, Mary had arrived, bearing news of some importance, she reckoned. It had been quite a while since they had last met up like this, as Sherry had just returned from a holiday in Malta.

"Where's Zareen, dear? And how was your trip?" asked Mary.

"She left a few days ago for a wedding in Bangalore. I don't expect she'll be back for another two days. It's great to see you, darling! I can't wait to hear what your news is. I must say, you've got me intrigued. First your news then my Malta news. Get yourself comfy; I'll be back in a jiffy."

Mary chose her favourite armchair, overlooking the garden. The magnolia trees were now in full bloom with their waves of creamy white flowers. The delphiniums and larkspurs were robust and splendid as they mixed and mingled in glorious hues of purple in the breeze, and even the birds of paradise were looking particularly majestic today. Mary sat back and soaked up the scenery, wondering just how these girls managed to keep the garden up to this standard. Goodness knows it was near impossible to get a gardener these days who knew a single thing about plants, let alone how to propagate them or what to do when there was an infestation!

Returning from the kitchen, Sherry sat on the sofa. "Mary, I can barely wait another minute, tell me what it is."

Leaning forward and sounding rather more dramatic than necessary, Mary said, "Sherry, you won't believe what happened last night. I heard all about it from Usha this morning. To start at the beginning, you did hear, didn't you, that AJ Panniker was in town?

"Apparently, that horrid idiot was found dead at the club last night. It seems to have been a heart attack or a stroke. He was found splayed out on top of his dinner in his room. Can you just imagine the sight of that, Sherry? He was at the club garden party yesterday. Really, you should have seen him... I mean, yes, I know, I've known him all his life. His mum was quite a nice lady actually, although how she stuck it out with that absurd husband of hers, I'll never know. The boy took after the dad for sure.

"As I was saying, you should have seen him at the party, my goodness, hobnobbing with all sorts of people who were way above his station in life. One of them was the Brigadier, no less! I, of all people, little old ME, had to go and rescue the poor man! AJ was making such an ass of himself. The poor Fonseca kids were just standing there listening to all his appalling plans for the development of their old home. I honestly felt like thumping him."

Mary had to sit back now and take a deep breath as she had said her piece all in one go.

Sherry took all this in with uncharacteristic glee. After all, such dramatic deaths hardly happen in Ooty, and certainly not in her circle of friends.

She knew AJ from many years ago, although he was a good decade younger than her. His shenanigans from the past crept into her thoughts. Quite the star athlete in his day, but he had always been such a show-off, even in his younger days. He hadn't grown out of it, from the sound of things.

"What did the police, doctor and all that lot have to say about it, though?"

"I don't think the police were involved at all, and the doctor said it was natural causes and I do believe, from my very reliable sources, that he had a heart problem of some sort."

"Mary, maybe this is just redemption, for the Pearls of life…"

"I think you're right, Sherry, like one of those 'laws of life'! After all, you and I know full well what a creep he was. Why he had to return here, I will never know."

Roast chicken sandwiches and chocolate cupcakes were washed down with steaming Glenmorgan tea. The drama of AJ's death had faded to the back of their minds as Sherry spoke of her holiday in Malta. She had gone there to attend the ordination of her best friend's son. Mary listened with fascination as story after story of the seminary, the priests, the food, the ceremony and, of course, of the spectacular sea views unfolded.

Long after Mary left, Sherry sat and thought about what she had heard. She chuckled as she recalled Mary saying 'way above his station in life'. In this day and age, one would never dream of uttering such an elitist phrase. But that was typical of Mary, whom Sherry concluded was a closet snob. She wondered what might or might not have really happened to AJ. She brushed aside any grim thoughts that came to mind. After all, she had known two men, much younger than AJ, who had dropped dead of heart attacks.

Am I so footloose and fancy free that I have to create a suspicious death just to keep myself occupied, she wondered, but try as she might, she just could not get the thought out of her head. Perhaps I'll go and nosey about the club. Knowing the staff, she believed that even with a 'normal' death on their hands, she would be given irresistible titbits about the late, colourful, and obnoxious AJ!

Chapter Five

Tears, Cheese and News

Watsonia

"You should have known. All these years! You were supposed to be managing the business! What the bloody hell were you thinking? How are we going to manage? There's no money now and we'll never be able to repay your father!" screeched Violet Fonseca at her husband. 'Fernhill Cheeses', his brainchild, was going under. She had gone along with the original business plan, hoping that this would be their fortune. She had always told Phyllis and their brother, Francis, not to worry about their futures. She would look after them after the debacle of Chater Hall, which left them virtually penniless. Her hopes and dreams were now falling apart.

Arun started towards her but changed his mind. The tall and slender Arun strode to the writing table, picked up a pipe and started filling it with his favourite tobacco. After this slow ritual, he began to light it, puffing hard and trying to push his worries away. The smoke lifted and trailed through the air. Lighting up was his way of dealing with life's problems or when he had to think particularly hard. He was now wondering what his next move should be.

Trying hard to appear in deep thought, he glanced at Violet. He remembered how she used to be when they began dating. Full of confidence and always full of life. Such a pretty thing, she had been. Shorter than her sister, but undoubtedly prettier. After twenty years, she had filled out considerably. He couldn't understand how she had managed to get herself into this dismal state. There were times when he wished he had said something, but it was too late now. He had to face the fact that his wife had turned into a rotund forty-year-old and their business was in the doldrums. How he longed to be away from this mess.

"Listen, it's not the end of the world. Dad has never asked us to repay the money and he certainly doesn't expect it. The factory is on prime land, Violet, smack on the edge of town, so we should get a huge amount for it. Think about it, things could be far worse. At least we have a roof over our heads, and we don't have children to educate."

"What?" shrieked Violet. "No children? How dare you say such a hurtful thing after all the miscarriages I've had?"

Arun's heart sank. He should have thought before he spoke.

"Sweetheart, I'm so sorry. That wasn't what I meant at all. All I mean to say is that we're not in dire financial straits. It pains me to see my beautiful wife in such a state, when there's no need to be."

Violet, however, was in tears once again. He knew the day had been set for nothing but wailing, accusations, and an endless flood of tears.

"Anyway, let's not let the maid hear. The last thing we need is for all and sundry to hear about this. We both know how the Ooty and Coonoor lot can be. Vile, once they get their teeth into nasty gossip."

Blowing her nose loudly, Violet stared at Arun. She squinted at him with hardened eyes. Large, hazel eyes which had once been filled with laughter, kindness, and mischief, now conveyed anger, mistrust, and frustration.

"You fool. Is that all you care about, what others think? You've never thought of us, have you? What were you doing all that time in the damn factory? And the money you spent on those courses, learning how to make those bloody cheeses?" screamed Violet, rage gripping her. "And what about that trip you made to Switzerland two years ago? Had you absolutely no clue as to what was going on in the market?"

Violet slumped into a chair, falling silent as she realised that she, too, hadn't foreseen the disaster that had unfolded. Some of the blame was on her, too. She knew this. And it was that fact which made it even harder for her to handle the devastating news. Perhaps some silence on her part now would be prudent before Arun, too, cottoned onto this and started accusing her of dual failure.

Arun, however, had been in charge of the business's operations, including its finances. Yet, he hadn't seen the market change, hadn't noticed that India had opened up to imports, not just for cheese, but all types of food. The consequence of which was that it wasn't as difficult as it once was to source the best cheeses from abroad. Thanks to just about everything being available now on the shelves, orders for Fernhill Cheeses were slowly, but steadily, drying up.

And Arun simply hadn't noticed. As long as he could hold onto contracts with the older stores in the area, he hoped to somehow bring the business back from the brink. Certainly, Fernhill Cheese was a good deal cheaper than the imports. There had been no need to tell Violet anything because he knew he could put it right. His real shortcoming was not realising Indians were far more sophisticated now than they were ten years ago. These days they were happy to pay for French and other European cheeses, because they wanted the real thing. His mind started to wander as he heard Violet sob again. Should he call her?

It would be easy to make his excuses, a trip to the accountant wouldn't go amiss. Getting his phone out of his pocket, he started to send off a message.

"Sweetheart, I had better go and see the accountant now. The sooner I get this all sorted out, the better for both of us. We can move on quicker. Will you be okay for a few hours?"

With her face still buried in her handkerchief, Violet didn't bother to look up.

Sighing, Arun made his way to the front door, grabbing his coat from the stand. He stopped in his tracks as his eye caught activity on the watsonia-lined drive; he frowned in frustration. This is the last thing I need now... he thought.

Quickly stepping up the front doorsteps and ignoring the blank look on Arun's face, his visitor exclaimed, "Well, well, dear man! A very good morning to you. Phyllis is still getting out of the car. We wanted to get to your place early so that we could break the news to you face to face."

Geoffrey never stood on ceremony. He walked straight in and slapped Arun affectionately on the back. Phyllis, in her usual graceful way, followed a moment after, looking stunning in high-heeled boots, a flared suede skirt, and beige shirt. She smiled brightly at her brother-in-law, swept past the two men, and walked into the sitting room.

Arun was taken aback with their arrival. Violet must have known but, as usual, she had not bothered to tell him, and, he guessed, with the shocking news that she got from him this morning, she must have forgotten. This was the last thing he needed, especially when he had just made other, very important plans.

As he closed the front door, he could hear Violet's nervous, excited voice making excuses to her sister for her appearance, telling Phyllis all about her sleepless night and the slight fever she had been running the evening before.

Arun rolled his eyes, knowing that he would have to repeat the same lies in a moment, but all these problems disappeared when he realised, with astonishment, what Geoffrey was batting on about. Geoffrey was regaling them about a death, a very unexpected death at that. Arun hurried behind him lest he missed any vital information.

Geoffrey was pacing up and down, while Phyllis stood by the large bay windows looking at Violet with a quizzical expression. Why on earth did her sister look like she'd just rolled out of the washing machine, she wondered. It couldn't just be due to her bad night, surely?

"… and so, we ran behind Rasheed; you know we really thought the waiter had been drinking or something. Can you imagine how shocking it was, seeing AJ dead, wine all over the floor? After all, we'd just been talking to him at the garden party although, I dare say, he was making a right ass

47

of himself, what with all his plans for Chater Hall. Don't you agree, darling?"

Leaving her spot at the bay window, Phyllis brushed past him, ignored his question, and sat next to her sister on the sofa. Violet would need hand holding now that Chater Hall had been dropped into the conversation. She made a mental note to tell Geoffrey that bringing up sensitive family matters when least expected was not a good idea. At all.

Oblivious to the discomfort of everyone around him, thick-skinned Geoffrey continued. "He wasn't exactly fit-looking, even though he clearly fancied himself. Frankly, I think he was just over-excited about being back and throwing his weight about at the party and his blood pressure just shot up. That's got to be it. Trouble is, no one has claimed the body. I rang poor Rasheed this morning to check if he was okay. After all he had to deal with last night, he looked like he needed a stiff drink and bed. He reckons the funeral will take place in the next couple of days."

Phyllis pushed up closer to her sister and rested one arm around her shoulder. Speaking softly, she lowered her head to meet Violet's and asked, "Do you need to see the doctor? You don't look good. Have you taken anything?"

Violet was beginning to look very pale indeed. She pushed herself upright, pulling her gown even more tightly around her generous frame. Smoothing out the wrinkles and folds of her clothes, she replied, "No, I'll be fine. It's just a sleepless night. A bit of rest today and I should be okay. What did you say AJ said about Chater?" Violet was totally oblivious to everyone staring at her. Wasn't she curious or bothered about AJ's death, they wondered? After all she was at the club just last night, the very night of his death, but no one wanted to worry her considering how poorly she looked.

Geoffrey, of course, was the only one who hadn't cottoned on. He launched further into his story.

"Now, I did like the old chap, bringing much needed entrepreneurship to the hills and all the rest of it. But he was getting up the backs of just about everyone at the party with his plans to convert Chater Hall into a shopping mall of some sort. Francis was there and you should have seen his face. Phyllis, darling, you looked pretty damned angry at him too. Don't blame any of you, after what AJ's father did, but as I've always said, let bygones be bygones. It's certainly not his fault, is it, if he came into his inheritance?"

Arun stood silently, soaking in this extraordinary news. He had heard about AJ's return but had not really had the time to see him. He and Violet couldn't make it to the garden party, as their factory manager was ill and Arun had to stand in. He lit his pipe and once again puffed trails of smoke into the air.

Geoffrey took a cigarette from his silver case and handed one to Phyllis, who by this time had had enough of Geoffrey. She was an expert at calming the waters. Lighting up, and sneaking a quick glance at Violet, she said softly, "Enough about Chater Hall. We don't need to know the details about what a dead man was planning, do we?"

With a sudden jolt, Violet jumped off the sofa, and, as if on stage, took up position at the unlit marble fireplace. She stood still and absently stared out above everyone's heads for a few seconds before turning around to face them. The room fell silent, and it did not escape her notice that they were all staring at her in expectation. They were not disappointed. She suddenly spoke, with a whine, "How dare that man even contemplate developing Chater? It's ours. It belongs to us. He knew we wanted it back and that we were prepared to make an offer, and he didn't have the decency to give us a sensible proposal. Poor Mama and Papa, what would they have thought about all this?" Much to everyone's dismay, she began to wail.

What a ridiculously sad sight she was now. The crow's nest had become partly undone and hung awkwardly, like a broken twig, on the side of her head. Her dressing gown had opened up and everyone noticed that her pyjama top buttons weren't matched up and one side of her shirt was all bunched up.

Arun, deciding it was high time he intervened and stopped this dismal spectacle, put his arms gently around Violet. He hated it when this property matter came up. They all took it so very personally. Speaking to her almost as one would speak to a child when explaining something which may upset them, he said, "There, there, my darling. He got what he deserved. Dead. Gone. At least we don't have to see his face again. As for Chater Hall, it's out of our hands now. We don't know who that property now goes to. He never had any kids that we know of, and I don't remember any close relatives."

Chapter Six

A Funeral That Happened

Under a weak and watery sun, Mary hurried along the pathway leading to St. Martin's Church. She was late. Her small, energetic figure resembled a cocoon, wrapped tightly in a black cashmere shawl. As usual, she had decided to walk. Walking was the one thing Mary knew kept her health on an even keel. At seventy-five, she definitely was not born into that generation of the gym goers of the nineties nor, for that matter, was she born into that generation of new age yoga lovers of the eighties. No, the key to Mary's robust health was plain, old-fashioned brisk walking and staying active!

As she made steady progress on the slight incline, she glanced fleetingly at the headstones on either side of the path, headstones that she knew only too well from the many years of attending service in this church. Some of the tombstones even belonged to close relatives, including that of her parents and a brother who had died as a child.

There were stones that seemed as if they were purposefully looming over you, judging you. Many more simply stood tall, looked uninterested, but were definitely superior in their manner!

For so many years, they had, in their numerous shapes and sizes, watched life go by in utter silence. They now knew it was time for another to join them as they watched those walking past them and into the large white building with the spire that presided grandly over the grounds.

"Mary!" shot out an urgent whisper. Sherry came into view as she took deep strides to catch up with her. She was already unbuttoning her duffle coat, desperately trying to cut short all the extra fussing before entering the church and settling down for the service. Sherry was also late for the funeral as there had been a car accident near her house. Being late to a funeral, of all events, was simply not in Sherry's book. She was pleased to see she was not the only one. Likewise, Mary, too, was pleased to see she wasn't the only one who was late. "Sherry, dear girl, I'm so glad to see you. I thought I was the only latecomer. You know, I was in two minds whether to attend but my conscience got the better of me. I really came for his mother's sake. She would have wanted me to be here." Mary thought it wiser to not mention that she also didn't wish to be the subject of gossip for her non-attendance as there were many in town who had admired this man. Better, she thought, to be cautious.

"Sometimes, Mary, we have to let bygones be bygones. AJ may have been a tiresome bully to those who came across him, but in death, we try to give thanks for life even though there might not be much for us to give thanks for. Just think, Mary, someone out there may well have received some kindness from him. Gosh! I'm sounding rather like the priest himself, aren't I?" Mary merely looked back at her in agreement.

As they entered the church, the congregation was reciting words they were all too familiar with, words from that Psalm that Protestants go back to time and time again when sending off their dead… their beloved Psalm number 23, "… though I walk through the valley of the shadow of death, I fear no evil…"

They looked around, deciding where they should take their seats. Shafts of soft light shone across at all angles through the lighter colours of the stained-glass windows, creating a striped design across the nave. Sherry noticed a ray hitting someone's bald and shiny head. She wondered whether he could actually feel the heat on his head.

The large church was half full, quite an achievement for AJ, in Sherry's opinion, considering he only really knew a handful of people here well. But she knew the real reason was that for most Indians, be it a funeral or a wedding, all those who were even vague acquaintances would expect to be present at such a milestone in a person's life. At least for funerals, they could turn up willy-nilly. For weddings, they would need an invitation, and, for sure, there would be dire consequences if the milkman or news agent was missed out on the invite list. As the service was well under way, they had to sit down quickly and quietly at the back of the church. Sherry noted that the church choir had also turned out in full strength.

They had just started singing 'Nearer My God To Thee', a hymn that reminded Sherry of far too many funerals past.

It had been a short, crisp service. Nothing like any funeral previously held in St. Martin's, at least not so far as Reverend Suresh could recall. No tears, no audible crying, and no handkerchiefs clutched by hands in anxious anticipation of flooding emotions. Once AJ's solicitors in Ooty confirmed that he had no remaining family, it had fallen on the Reverend to make all the funeral arrangements. He had never known AJ or his parents, who had worshipped in this church decades before he had been transferred to St. Martin's, but he had felt it now his duty to make some effort for this man taken by God in such an untimely way. There would be no wake, although, in recognition of the need for people to share memories, he announced to the congregation that they could mingle on the grounds after the burial to exchange memories of AJ.

The burial was short, too. It was enriched somewhat by a few who were humming the last hymn of the service, 'Abide With Me'. Obviously, they couldn't get the tune out of their heads. Sherry wasn't surprised; it was in her head as well, such meaningful words and such a moving tune, too.

After the burial, the ladies made their way outside to the church lawn where the young and energetic Reverend Suresh had put out chairs and tables. The most the church could muster up was steaming coffee and simple cheese sandwiches, but it obviously sufficed. Everyone was soon clutching a cup as they munched on their sandwiches. It was certainly a very plain affair compared to what AJ would have anticipated. There were a number of familiar faces, including Ali Rasheed, who always made a point of demonstrating his respect for past and present members of the club. Francis Fonseca and Pearl were greeting each other with nods. Ali moved closer to them.

Sherry approached them quickly.

"Good morning, Ali, Francis, Pearl. I was really not sure who would be here today. It was a simple and fitting funeral, don't you think?" Sherry was usually adept at eliciting conversation and today she was keen to hear any opinions about AJ.

Pearl was the first to reply, although not quite in the way that anyone had anticipated. She let out a deep sigh.

"Simple and fitting indeed, I fully agree, Sherry," she said. "When you come to think of it, he might very well have been my brother-in-law. That is, if Avril hadn't died. Who knows? It might have worked out in the end, and she might have had a very comfortable life. It's their karma. There's no point in wishing this or that had happened. What's happened, happened, because that's what was going to happen."

As everyone absorbed her unexpected reply, at the same time thinking they hadn't ever heard the word 'happened' repeated so many times in one sentence, Ali interjected, "Sometimes people just go like that, for no reason. He obviously had a heart attack. Many people go at a young age, anyway. Let's not dwell on it. He would have been an asset to the club if he had lived but, sadly, that was not to be."

Ali wondered why he was talking such tosh, as if everyone in their small group didn't already know what an obnoxious guest AJ had been.

Sherry gazed at Ali. He was looking quite despondent. It must be the aftermath of the unpleasant way that AJ died and the palaver of the discovery. She wondered, if it had simply been the case of a portly club member dropping dead on the golf course in the middle of the day, that it would be quite 'par for the course' for Ali... "excuse the pun, Sherry," she told herself with a chuckle.

Yes, it must definitely be AJ's death. That, clubbed with having to organise the upcoming Equestrian Ball, is what's tiring him out. God knows the organising of that massive event can knock the stuffing out of anyone. She knew that along with all this, there had been some trouble with the club staff, most of whom possessed that universal tendency of the unsophisticated, which is to make an unnecessary fuss and drama about any untimely death.

I must tell him that I'll be helping out with the Ball. It'll certainly perk him up and ease his mind, Sherry decided. Such was her supreme confidence that her presence would be all soothing.

Chapter Seven

The Dawn

Thanks to the sharp afternoon light, Dimple squinted across the vast lawn with great difficulty at her daughters. Unlike her older set of twins, these two were going to be quite the handful for some time to come, she realised.

Koko and Kiki were giggling hysterically at a young man who was obviously relating a hilarious story. She decided to leave them be. At just nineteen years old, Dimple's second set of twin girls were rather silly things, taking much of their privileged life for granted. It must be said, though, that their mother didn't make much of an effort to get them to see the reality of life around them. She once shrugged when a dear friend gently prodded her on the subject, simply saying, "It's their destiny, darling. Why should they worry about all the suffering in the world when others are so terribly keen to do so?" This is not to say that Dimple was a frightful selfish horror. She was, in fact, kind and gentle. She did, however, enjoy life thoroughly and deemed it her children's rite of passage to do so, too.

Smiling to herself, she decided to get back to her latest acquisition, an antique crystal bowl. It caught the afternoon sunlight flooding into the room and reflecting thousands of sparkling stars off the bowl. Dimple carried it by its gold handles and carefully placed it where it belonged. Gently closing the glass cabinet door, she locked it with a satisfying click and stepped back to admire its beauty.

Miki would be back soon, and that meant tea would be laid out now. Miki Ponnappa was Dimple's husband, the largest proprietary planter in south India. Miki's empire covered coffee, tea, and rubber.

All his estates were inherited from his playboy father, Jojo. Although his plantations were far flung, and each estate had its own beautiful 'owners' bungalow, it was on the outskirts of Ooty town that the family made its home. Their Ooty property, named The Dawn, stood on one of the most picturesque parts of The Nilgiris, the Wenlock Downs. The property once used to be the Ootacamund Equestrian Society. The Society building stood smack in the middle of twenty acres of land. The back end of the property was taken up with stables and the front was mostly lawn and garden with tall, regal, evergreen cypress and monkey puzzle trees planted in groups.

The land and buildings were snapped up by Miki's father for a song, thirty years ago when the Society wound down. One side of the property had a spectacular abundance of gloriously blooming golden yellow gorse and broom, brought over by the Raj when they were so eager to change the vast Nilgiris landscape to match that of their beloved Scotland.

Stepping out into the garden, her soft pashmina shawl draped around her shoulders, Dimple watched as tea was being laid out on the wrought iron table, under the largest monkey puzzle tree. The vibrant golden hues of evening sunlight caught the highlights in her short curly hair, creating a fetching but slightly comical looking halo.

Seeing Miki's car zip up the driveway, Dimple's mind went back to when they first met, under the oddest of circumstances, in a London hospital car park of all places! Dimple grew up in England, but her family were originally from the Punjab. Her father was a doctor with the NHS, and it was in the same hospital where her father worked that they met. She was waiting to pick her dad up, when Miki and a friend of his arrived in a car which bumped into hers and the rest, as they say, is history. For Miki and Dimple, it was love at first sight.

She strolled outside and poured a cup of her favourite Earl Grey tea. Familiar footsteps could be heard approaching along the patio.

Dimple looked towards the walkway, "Hi, darling, how was your day?"

"Okay, there was not much progress with the labour officer in Peechi," replied Miki as he gave her a peck on her forehead. He sat back in his chair, grateful for the cup of tea he was handed, and said, "Before you tell me what you've been up to, and before I forget, I bumped into Sherry in town. She started telling me about what happened at the club a few days ago. I just can't understand why is it that whenever we go out of town for a couple of days, we always hear stories of all sorts going on in this small town? Nothing ever happens when we're here. Apparently, some fella that everyone seems to have known from the past, turned up out of the blue from England. Anyway, it seems he met up with loads of people at the garden party and later that night was found dead. He was only in his forties, it seemed. He was staying at the club as well. So, what do you make of that then?"

"Trust us to have missed the party, but anyway, who was he?"

"She mentioned the name, but I can't for the life of me remember. Certainly not anyone we know, and, in any case, she said he had only just returned from the U.K. Only back for three days and then, wham, dead!"

So typical of him not to bother to remember the chap's name, Dimple thought. She wondered if she ought to suggest he puts on a hat, his bald head was bound to get too much sun and then, for sure, a headache would start, but then, he was so touchy about his hair loss. She finally decided to keep quiet; it was just too tiring trying to advise a sensitive sixty-year-old on what to do. Instead she went back to the dead man. "I'll call Sherry later to commiserate. Zareen's not in town otherwise I could have sorted a tennis game with her."

Miki was quite oblivious of her exasperation, as he was now frowning at the ruckus at the far end of the lawn.

"What those two see in that silly boy, I have no idea. He's as ridiculous as that lazy father of his."

Dimple decided to ignore the noise from the other end of the lawn and plunged into what was, according to her, the pressing subject of the moment, that of the upcoming Equestrian Ball that they were organising. It was a huge event, to be held at the Ootacamund Country Club. An exclusive evening of cocktails, dinner, and dancing, admission to which was restricted by the sale of a limited number of tickets. A good chunk of the proceeds went towards the upkeep of the highly bred show horses, stabled at the club, following the demise of the Equestrian Society. Almost all of them were descended from the horses that were originally kept at The Dawn.

For the Ponnappas, their contribution to the Ball was a tribute to the daily life that was once the mainstay of their property, and it was one that they could well afford. For all their glitziness, the Ponnappas were respectful of history and had found that gestures such as organising the Equestrian Ball were, surprisingly, personally fulfilling.

This was their third year of organising this event and Dimple was determined that this year, it would be perfect, having had the opportunity now to iron out two years of the glitches they had experienced.

"Darling, I'm meeting Bunny tomorrow about the catering. She said Sherry is going to help her and we've decided that the best people to cater are the Screwallahs as they did a really good job last year and, of course, they need the business badly, thanks to the Gina problem, poor things."

Miki grunted his agreement, thinking to himself, all this is best left to these ladies.

Chapter Eight

Sherry's Chance

The receptionist's smile made her shudder. Firmly gripping her room key, Sherry made her way to her room. Before her, the long dark corridor seemed to snake away into nothingness. She simply couldn't see the end of it; laughter swept up the grand staircase, she knew it was just the party downstairs, nothing to be alarmed about.

The corridor suddenly narrowed into a dingy tunnel. She looked around frantically, but she absolutely couldn't find her room, none of the doors had numbers. Claustrophobia started building up quickly. A ghastly smell travelled through the air, tailing a silhouette which suddenly came into view. As it got closer, it began to run towards her, screaming, with its arms outstretched. Sherry turned to escape but there was nowhere to go. Gripped with panic, she grabbed a door handle and struggled to open it. It just would not open, no matter how hard and how much she tried. She heard a strangled wail behind her. Overpowered with fear, she turned once more. The silhouette lay on the floor, but before she could understand what was happening, the door behind her creaked open. A hand shot out and grabbed her by her hair, pulling fiercely...

Sherry opened her eyes and quickly sat up. The pale dawn light peered through the curtains.

As she rubbed her cold arms, she realised that she had had an awful nightmare. It was rare for her to have horrible dreams. She was generally a sound sleeper and certainly never remembered her dreams, but the feel of that vicious hand yanking at her hair felt, at the very moment she opened her eyes, so real.

Her mouth was dry. Reaching for her glass of water, she tried hard to recall the details of the dream, but they were quickly receding. Yet it seemed to have opened a door, letting into her mind a nagging feeling that something was not right about the manner of AJ's death.

The mellow chimes of the clock downstairs nudged her out of bed. It was only six o'clock, and although Sherry usually rose at seven to a tea tray brought to her by Philomena, she decided to make it an early start. There was a lot to think about and she wanted to catch Zareen before she caught up with the day.

"So, what do you think, Zareen?"

Sherry wanted her opinion on her hunch that maybe there was a chance that AJ had not met a natural end. Zareen had been sceptical at first as Sherry recounted her suspicions while they tucked into bacon and eggs.

"It's possible, but who on earth would want to go so far as to kill him?" asked Zareen.

Sherry was a little exasperated at this point. Zareen was not seeing things with the same clarity as she did.

"Well, think about it, Zee Zee… just pass me the coffee, dear. So many people here have every reason to begrudge his return and all this talk about his antics at the garden party the other day could easily have tipped someone over the edge."

She looked at Zareen for some understanding, at the same time realising this was definitely not the right time to tell her she ought to really make an effort to lose the weight she had recently gained. Zee had definitely let herself go these last couple of years, could also be the blasted menopause…

Sherry was shaken out of her wandering thoughts as Zareen decided that she should now take the 'situation' firmly in hand.

"If that were true, then maybe the matter is better left as it is. You don't want to end up a dead body because someone got the wind up. You know what they say, Sherry, once they've killed, the second murder is easy. And who the heck knows? This could be the 'enth murder by this person. If it was a murder at all, and it absolutely isn't. You can take it from me, after all, I know about these things. I've seen this sort of thing happen God knows how many times. People die. That's it. And anyway, Sherry, you don't know a thing. It's all hunches and feelings with you and that's probably because you don't have much to do right now. And you don't need me to tell you this sort of thing isn't a game. If you're so sure something's up, oughtn't you to be going to the police about it?" Goodness, thought Sherry, typical of Zee Zee to not hold back! She knew that she was not going to get much further with her.

Tiffany, lying on the dhurrie next to the dining table, cocked her head to one side and looked up at Sherry with her big, sympathetic eyes. Sherry smiled at her, knowing that Tiffany was on her side. Sherry perked up and decided to hit step one of the plan, which she had meticulously put together before breakfast and deliberately failed to mention to Zareen.

She had promised Bunny that she would help coordinate with the caterers for the ball next week. It was at the country club so it would give her an opportunity to hang around the club and get a feel of the whole dismal episode.

The thought of chatting with the sunny Bunny Fussington made her smile, for the first time that morning. She resolutely picked up the phone and, after the usual niceties, she offered to take charge of the food layout for the Equestrian Ball, a thankless task that Bunny was happy to relinquish as she was far more interested in spending time on the details of the canapés and such, especially as this year they had planned to replicate an historical menu with the Screwallahs.

Sherry was beginning to feel more herself. After the horrid start to the morning, everything was finally falling into place nicely. She now had a jolly good excuse to go to the club, so she decided to call ahead and fix a time to meet Ali.

The driveway up towards the clubhouse was extremely wide, wide enough to take three lane traffic, Sherry hazarded. Honestly, in the 1800s, they certainly had no reason to save space!

She had always loved this short drive up towards the club. On one side, for almost as far as one could see, there was an immaculate green meadow and on the other side, in sharp contrast, were dense thickets of short trees. Known as shola trees, they are a photographer's dream with their gnarled trunks and curved branches covered with bright green moss. Most of the trees had stunning orchids popping out at odd angles. Shola trees are rare, for they are made up of a mere twenty odd varieties and they have almost died out, thanks to the dangerous proliferation of eucalyptus imported by the British.

Reaching the top of the drive, she veered off into a side lane, lined with rose bushes, leading down to the club car park.

Jumping out of her car and with a light spring to her step, Sherry entered the club and almost smashed smack into Daniel, a long serving club employee. She kicked herself. She was always doing this, because as soon as she would enter, her eyes would be shocked by the contrast of the brightness outside and the dark interior of the club lobby. Everything would be pitch dark for a few seconds until her eyes became accustomed to the dimness. Couldn't they just put brighter lights in the lobby, she thought, quite irritated.

As she had called in advance to get an appointment with the secretary, Daniel whom she had almost crashed into, told her that he knew about the meeting and said that the secretary had suggested they sit down at 'The Buttery', the well-loved breakfast room. He also apologised to her on behalf of the secretary, who was running a bit late.

Settling down with her pen and papers, she glanced around her. The room was bright and the arrangements of white and yellow daisies on all the tables seemed to be bobbing their heads in the sunlight and smiling at her.

At one end of the room, a young man was being discreetly trained on how to lay a table. He was dressed in a brand-new uniform. Life goes on, she thought.

Sherry felt warm and happy. Daniel was hovering. She seized her chance and casually mentioned 'the death'. As expected, she was met with an enthusiastic, albeit abridged, version of what happened on the night of AJ's death. Daniel, whose name was pronounced Denial by all the staff and indeed by all his friends too, was acutely aware that his boss could well turn up earlier than expected and would not appreciate his indiscretion!

"Who actually found the body, Daniel?" she asked.

"Bartho-lo-mew, ma'am," he replied, pushing his chest up slightly.

"Poor chap. Is he very upset or has he recovered?"

She had known both Daniel and Bartholomew since they had joined the club, donkey's years ago, as kitchen helpers. They had both worked themselves up the ranks and were now very proud waiters. She smiled at him as she looked into his kind eyes, remembering how she always referred to them as 'the long and the short of it' as Daniel barely came up to Bartholomew's shoulder.

"Yes, ma'am. He's still very upset. He didn't expect to find him dead on his food like that, you see, ma'am."

Well, of course he didn't, she thought.

"Have they taken away all Mr Panniker's belongings, Daniel?"

As he was about to reply, the secretary strode in, and Daniel scuttled away. Ali looked as tired as he did at the funeral two days ago. She decided he would probably appreciate talking about the aftermath of the body's discovery before going into the nitty-gritty details of the upcoming event.

"How are you after all this awfulness, Ali?" she asked gently as he settled down on the chair opposite her. She noticed that he had recently had a very short haircut and his pepper and salt hair was now standing upright. His reading glasses were jammed down firmly on the bridge of his nose and his eyes looked tired. Sherry had a soft spot for him, for he always came across to her as a lonely figure.

"Well for starters, no one liked him, Sherry. He was boorish and thought too much of himself, but I never thought he would drop dead like that; Bartholomew was hysterical. I've never seen a grown man behave so ridiculously."

Sherry seized her chance.

"Oh, dear, Ali. How much of your time is going on this, apart from the arrangements for the ball? Can I do anything at all to help? You see, I knew AJ before he left for England; I can organise all his stuff and pack it away for storage if you like. I can start now. I've got loads of time on my hands and as you've got a lot on your plate right now, I can come back again in a few days for this meeting," finished Sherry, feeling hopeful that Ali would agree to her rather breathless suggestion.

"You see, the thing is, we locked the room door after Dr Zachariah examined him and said we could remove the body. He said no autopsy was needed. So, the body was taken away and the room has remained locked ever since. No one's told me what to do with his things. Certainly no one's claimed them, and I have no idea where to send them,

Sherry. And we have a full house starting next week," he finished, looking glum.

This was the first time that Sherry was given the name of the doctor who examined AJ's body. She hadn't even thought of enquiring earlier. Stupid of me, she thought. Maybe Zareen hit the nail on the head with her mini tirade this morning. Maybe she really was just flailing about as she had nothing to do.

"Don't worry, Ali. I'll list out everything and pack it all up. I'll store it all, including the car, at Buxey and I'll put out ads in the papers and put it on Facebook to say his personal items are available to any bona fide relative or friend who would like them. If no one has come forward at the end of six months, we'll give them to charity."

She continued, "It was mentioned at his funeral that his local lawyers were McQueen & Ramdas. We can put it to them to get the go ahead. What do you think, Ali?"

"I think it's a good idea, especially as I don't see what other course of action can be taken and, yes please, Sherry, I would much rather meet up in a couple of days on the food matter. I just don't feel really settled since this death. You know, we had to tell Bartholomew to take a week off work and rest. I mean, honestly, some of the staff now say they don't want to go into that room as it's cursed. It's the silliest thing I've heard as nothing has ever happened in that room before. It's all quite draining, you know."

Sadly, for Ali Rasheed, Sherry was no longer concentrating on his moaning. She was just so delighted to have got the doctor's name, a name she knew well and someone she knew she would soon be meeting.

Chapter Nine

From the Same Pot

Arun looked at Francis unapologetically and slightly challengingly, then realising there was nothing much the mild-mannered Francis was going to throw back at him, he looked back down at his whiskey.

They were sitting in Francis's home, which was a cottage he rented in Mary Mendoza's compound. Francis had moved there when he came back to The Nilgiris after his early retirement from the army. As a young man away from his hometown and posted in far flung corners of India, he had always imagined his home would be Chater Hall when he returned, but now he was stuck in this rented cottage. It's not that it was too bad. It just wasn't what he had imagined his retirement dwelling would be.

Lt. Col. Francis Fonseca appraised his brother-in-law through shrewd eyes. Soft hearted and affable at first glance, Francis was, nevertheless, a classic case of not judging a book by its cover. He was, in fact, regarded as smart, quick thinking, and decisive by his fellow officers. They were, of course, the ones who knew him best.

Francis sighed after hearing the sad story of yet another business having gone down the tube. He wasn't by nature an accusatory type of chap but in this instance, he did feel that Arun had quite clearly taken his eye off the ball.

Although he had heard rumours that Arun was carrying on with someone else, it wasn't a subject he was interested in, despite Violet being his sister. He had, however, no doubt that this added distraction hadn't helped Arun's concentration.

Recalling the Chater Hall blow the Fonseca family had received some years before and now hearing this discouraging story, Francis was upset, but for his sisters mainly. He would be all right. He received a jolly good amount in monthly pension from the army. Phyllis may well get a decent pension too, but Violet would be left in the lurch for sure, especially if this nincompoop left her. Francis had always suspected that Arun married her only because she was part heir to the huge Chater Hall property.

In the minds of the Fonseca children, although never really discussed amongst them, the understanding was that after their parents' time they would redevelop the property and, as part of the deal, each get a cottage of their own. Goodness knows that the five acres could easily allow for this. Unfortunately, their dreams all came crumbling down when their father, John Fonseca, fell heavily into debt. He had borrowed money to invest in a teak farm, which turned out to be a massive scam, and had lost his entire investment. This was all very well except for the fact that the person who John Fonseca borrowed from turned out to be a nasty character. The atmosphere started to feel dangerous and, with a wife and three children to take care of, John, in an effort to contain the situation, quickly pledged the Chater Hall land and home to Gopal Panniker, AJ's father, and in return received the huge amount he needed to repay the loan. Gopal Panniker was known in the district to be quite the swashbuckling real estate tycoon, although little did the general population realise that he was as far from a tycoon as one could be. In India, there is a belief that some people have a 'lucky hand' and, conversely, there are others who are deemed 'unlucky'. Gopal was, sadly and firmly, in the unlucky category. Try as he might, many of the businesses he took over went downhill for no apparent reason.

John Fonseca was a diligent man. He and his wife, Agnes, scraped and saved and paid off most of the debt to Gopal, although it took several years. Sadly though, by the time they were on the home run, they suffered another setback. John required chemotherapy for throat cancer and payments were delayed by almost eight months.

They got over this too and, being naive, very much hoped that Gopal Panniker would overlook the couple of extra months now needed for them to make the last few payments. Shockingly, this was not to be. Gopal seized the land with the beautiful home that had sheltered the Fonseca family for four generations.

As if this tragic situation were not enough, the aftermath of the 'land grab', as the Fonseca siblings called it, saw their darling mother fall into deep depression and their father's cancer resurge, ravaging his body. Sadly, both died within a few months of each other. She of heart failure, and he from the cancer. It was a wonder that their children, who by then were young adults about to sally forth into the big wide world, were able to get through this second tragedy.

Francis and his sisters knew that everyone in town thought the property had been sold and they let them believe it. It was much better than the embarrassment of the miserable story being known to all and sundry.

Gopal Panniker also died soon after their parents. It seemed almost like biblical redemption in their eyes. It was short lived redemption, though, as Gopal left Chater Hall to his only child, AJ Panniker.

Francis was pulled out of these maudlin thoughts by Arun asking, "What do you think is going to happen now that this Panniker chap has died?"

"Well, nothing much. Certainly, Chater won't come back to us unless we buy it back, which is impossible for us."

"Don't you think there could be some way we can go through the courts, plead for some kind of understanding that there was only two months left to pay back? I mean, just think about it, Francis. If you all got Chater Hall back, it would make all the difference to our lives."

Francis not only noted the word 'our', but also ignored Arun's suggestion. Speaking more to himself, he said, "I was at the club the night he died."

"Oh, you never said that earlier. Were you there during that hullabaloo Geoffrey told us about?"

"No, no, I was long gone by then. Mary, as always, was having her dinner there and it started raining so I thought I would pick her up. I parked and popped in to tell her I would wait for her in the car. I misjudged the timing. The poor thing was just tucking into her soup so I knew it would be a bit of a wait. I wasn't properly dressed for the club anyway, otherwise I would have joined the others for a drink while she finished."

All Francis got in reply from Arun was, "Eating her soup, was she? You do realise that her soup and the soup he drowned in must have come out of the same pot?"

Chapter Ten

Lady Fussington and the Screwallahs

Driving through Ooty town, Bunny Fussington realised how frightfully pleased she was. She had truly made the right decision to come to India. The onslaught of colours, noise, and chaotic traffic was enough to re-energise anyone, no matter how energetic or sprightly one was in the first place!

When she made the decision to move to India, she knew that she was leaving the glorious homes she had shared with James for twenty-three years, but she also realised life in England, hopping from one beautiful property to the other as the seasons changed, would never be the same without him.

She and James were so much in love, so connected to each other, a tendency so common amongst childless couples. After James had died so suddenly and peacefully in his armchair the previous year, the property and title went to his nephew, the new Lord Halford Fussington. Bunny was offered her own home on the property by dear affectionate Halford, but she just simply couldn't stand the sight of his second wife, Suzanne, who had ruined Halford's first marriage to the lovely Lucy.

Suzie was a real gold digger, if ever there was one. Halford, like all men, was unbelievably stupid when it came to women. He just couldn't for the life of him see a scheming minx standing in front of him. What a messy divorce it turned out to be too, with all sorts of stories being made up by the tabloids. Poor Lucy. She was heartbroken to have lost her ally, Bunny, to India, but when the time came to say goodbye, Lucy had somewhat recovered. She cheerfully announced that she would come to stay for the winter. Bunny knew it was going to be a lovely Christmas.

So, Bunny left her beloved England for India. She had, some years previously, inherited a lovely little house in Ooty from her aunt, Elvira Thompson. Elvira had lived in Ooty for many years and was a renowned landscape painter. Needless to say, the stunning views and extremely varied seasons in The Nilgiris were enough to keep Elvira firmly rooted. This is something to be said, as before her arrival on these mountains, Elvira had been quite the rolling stone, never settling for more than a year or so in any of her chosen destinations.

Here in India, Bunny could easily afford domestic staff and a chauffeur. She insisted on calling her driver, Dilip, 'the chauffeur' although in India, they were simply called 'drivers'. As her liveried 'chauffeur' drove deftly through the bustling town centre, en route to the Screwallah home and office, Bunny settled back and admired the blue monogram on the back of his cap. Halford was really a darling boy, for he had allowed her to use the Fussington coat of arms for her staff in India, and in return she promised him that she would never ever ferry her staff about the world!

Sighing happily, Bunny pulled her mind back to the matter on hand, which was the recreating of a menu from a 1965 Equestrian Ball. Frankly speaking, the 1965 menu was the earliest menu she and Dimple could find from the club's archives. They had so hoped to find something from the '50s, but it didn't really matter much as the '65 menu was an excellent one.

Arriving at the large Screwallah compound, simply known as 'The Kitchen', Bunny stumbled awkwardly over ducks and chickens as they scurried past her. The soft ground was also slushy, as a result of the rain last night. Her shoes kept sinking into the wet ground as she made her way. With some difficulty, she arrived at the largest of the three buildings on the property, looking rather the worse for wear thanks to the mud all over her shoes.

The door was opened by the tall and handsome Adam, Anna and Aiden Screwallah's son.

"Adam, dear boy, how are you?" she asked as she gave him an appraising look.

"I'm good thanks, Bunny. Mum is all ready for you."

Adam took Bunny down past the side of the house to the Screwallah office. Anna was just putting coffee on for the three of them.

"Darling, how are you? I can't thank you and Dimple enough for giving us this job," Anna said as she hugged Bunny warmly.

"Gosh, Anna, I don't think there's anyone near as good as you all are for a job like this and remember how brilliantly it turned out last year?" replied Bunny with an encouraging grin.

She sat down, on what she soon realised, was quite an uncomfortable wooden chair. An absolutely enormous sepia toned photograph of a young Parsi man looked straight down onto Bunny. He wore the traditional Parsi hat, the pagdi, and had an ever so slightly amused look about him, as if to say 'because you're insisting, I'm sitting for you!' There was no doubt in Bunny's mind that he was a grandfather or maybe even a great grandfather of Aiden's. Fidgeting slightly, Bunny thought that she had better first ask after the rest of the family. After all, she was a newcomer to this town and must develop and forge firm friendships if she were to enjoy a good, secure life here.

"Anna, first tell me how you all are. How is Aiden and how is Gina doing?"

In response, Anna took a quick look around. Adam was now missing.

"Bunny, I know we haven't known each other for long, but I feel I can trust you. I think something's up with Aiden. Frankly, I think he's either having an affair or is up to something strange. He just doesn't look himself at all these days and he keeps popping out at odd times and doesn't come back for hours on end. I'm worried sick."

Bunny certainly didn't expect to hear this. She was stumped for an appropriate reply and didn't want to put her foot in it either. She tried hard to think quickly but found herself terribly distracted by Anna's eyes; why on earth did Anna insist on using bright blue mascara? It simply did not 'go' with her very pale skin and jet-black hair. Taking a deep breath, she pulled herself back to the task of finding an appropriate response. Bunny decided to take the safe route and plunged into a bright and positive scenario.

"Look, Anna, don't think about anything negative. There could be a hundred reasons why he's going out and it could all be innocent. Men are proud creatures, Anna; if you want my advice, I'd say just leave it be for some time. See how long it carries on before you start to really worry."

"I suppose you're right, but I just can't figure it out. I don't need this extra worry with the shocking news of what we got a few months ago. I'm not sure if you heard about it though, Bunny?" asked Anna in a strained voice.

"No, I don't think so," said Bunny with some trepidation. What on earth was Anna going to swing at her now? she wondered.

Looking as if tears may well up any minute now, Anna started to explain with a tremor to her voice, "Well, as you know, Gina has been in a wheelchair ever since a horrible car crash six years ago. The accident was right here in Ooty. She was so bad, we thought we would lose her." Anna stopped at this point and wiped away tears before they ran down her face and made a mess. "Thank God, she pulled through bu... bu... but her legs just didn't get sorted, Bunnyeeee," Anna finished with a wail. She looked miserable.

Bunny made the appropriate sympathetic sounds and noticed that Adam was still missing.

Coffee had been mixed and served. Taking a much-needed sip, Anna continued, "She settled well after the accident, Bunny, she really did. But two months ago, we received a legal letter saying that the shortcut she... and we for that matter, but of course we don't matter so much, is now no longer available for us." She sniffed again.

By now, Bunny wondered whether she should have just plunged right into the business at hand, but quickly brushing this uncharitable thought aside, she looked at Anna questioningly.

Taking her cue from Bunny and realizing that she may have no idea of what she was on about, Anna continued, "You see, the next property to ours is Chater Hall. The house was built a hundred years ago by an Armenian from Calcutta and, to cut a long story short, the Fonseca family owned it for a few generations. They suddenly sold it lock, stock, and barrel to some unknown man from England, which is all very well…"

She was sniffling again, but the hot coffee was helping her along.

"The legal letter we got said that we can't any more use the shortcut through the Chater Hall property that gets us into the centre of town in a jiffy."

"Oh gosh, Anna. So, you mean Gina was using this shortcut, too?"

"Yes, Bunny, and it's only because of this shortcut that Gina was able to get that job at the jewellery shop." She looked even more miserable now.

"Can't you write and ask, Anna?" was Bunny's weak response.

"Noooooo," she whined, "because the new owner turned out to be that chap who died at the club, so I don't know what's going to happen now that he's gone."

She looked at Bunny keenly for a few moments before saying, in a conspiratorial tone, "We saw him at the club on the same day he died." Anna nodded at Bunny with a satisfied and somewhat knowing look and then leant forward, before continuing.

"We were right there at the club when they found the body that night. It was all so frightful, Bunny. We'd gone there earlier in the morning, Aiden and I, to deliver the food for the garden party and I took the dogs too, for a good run. They tripped a man over and it was all such a mess. Anyway, we returned at night to pick up our containers from the club kitchen when an almighty racket started. I heard later on that the chap who fell over the dogs was the same man who had died in his room when we were there and that he's the same man who bought Chater Hall. And now he's dead so there's no one left for us to ask, is there?"

Finishing off the last dregs of her coffee Anna said, "Although with him dead, I can't imagine anyone would now still insist on closing off the shortcut for us. Apparently, he was planning a huge redevelopment of Chater Hall which is why the whole area was to be closed off to people like us."

Bunny thought this through and decided to take the positive route once again.

"I think that now the whole project will probably never take off, Anna. After all, there's no one to spearhead it with this chap dead."

Anna suddenly got a wild look in her eyes and, ignoring Bunny's encouraging reply, she asked in a high-pitched voice, "Bunny, do you think he died because he was pushed by the dogs? He had a really hard fall, you know. Dozens of people saw it. He may have hurt his head without realizing it. Ooooh my, this is another sin our family will have to live with on top of whatever the sin was that's ruined our darling girl's life forever!"

Appalled, Bunny couldn't for the life of her think what to say now. This was all just too 'Indian' for the very British girl that she was... and that boy Adam was STILL missing. But, as she struggled to get an appropriate word out, she was saved by a violent knocking on the front door. It was Violet Reddy, looking red-eyed and tired.

Bunny sighed. She knew now this visit was going to be a very long haul.

Chapter Eleven

It's a Case Of 'Either/Or'

"Zareen, what are you wearing tonight?" asked Sherry.

"I don't know, and I don't feel like going either. I'm sooooo exhausted after all that gardening today," said Zareen as she lounged on the sofa with her grateful feet resting on the coffee table.

"Oh, pleeeeese come. It won't be the same without you, Zee Zee," pleaded Sherry.

"I'll see… what time is it?" asked Zareen grudgingly.

"Seven, and it's only drinks and a casual chat to tie up loose ends for the ball. We'll be back by nine at the latest."

"Okay, I'll try, but you know, Sherry, pruning those hydrangeas is VERY difficult. You should try it one day. Just try getting your secateurs in between those giant flower heads. It's not easy. I've got scratches all over my arms."

Her tone didn't sound too congenial, or hopeful, thought Sherry, but it was what it was. She was looking forward to this little get-together as she knew Dr Danny Zachariah was going to be there and he was the medical officer who gave the verdict on AJ's death.

The party was at Dimple's. Miki wouldn't be there, sadly. As always, he was at one of his far-flung estates, no doubt sorting out never-ending labour problems or the acute shortage of labour that all these plantations were experiencing these days. Miki was an entertaining host, often having his guests in stitches all evening. She would miss him this evening.

When the time came, Zareen's mood had changed for the better and she decided to make a go of the evening and enjoy herself. The Ponnappas were actually friends with Zareen first, long before they had met Sherry. Zareen had helped Dimple some years ago to nurse the younger twins when the household came down with both mumps and chicken pox at the same time.

Sherry was driving. It wasn't a long way to The Dawn, fifteen minutes at the most. In that sense, Ooty town was small. It was only getting to the outlying tea estates that could take more than an hour or so. It was a bright evening with a gigantic bright moon lighting the way for them.

Dimple opened the front door. That was the nice thing about her. Posh as she was, she ignored certain rituals that many of the nouveau riche clung onto for dear life, such as having staff open the door to guests. She looked absolutely gorgeous. Hugging her, Sherry said, "Take a step back, sweetie, so we can take it all in."

Dimple looked stunning indeed, dressed in an embroidered sage green salwar with the luxurious, inimitable Sue London flats firmly on her feet and numerous delicate Gillian Finlay necklaces and bracelets glistening around her neck and wrists. She was certainly a sight for sore eyes.

The Ponnappa home was also a sight to behold, beautiful and plush. In fact, one would expect no less, given the impressive driveway and lawns they would have to pass through before arriving at the mansion.

Intricately designed carpets from all parts of the world were on the floors. Beautiful paintings adorned the walls, including a few Elvira Thompson masterpieces of the Wenlock Downs.

Dimple had two smartly uniformed 'houseboys', as they are called in India, serving short eats and drinks to the guests. What a lovely, privileged life Dimple led, thought Sherry. And lucky us to be a part of it. The thing about Dimple was that she always did things absolutely pukka when she entertained. Casual entertaining or formal, her guests could expect the best in food and service from her rather larger than necessary domestic 'team', as Dimple referred to them. Dimple's older twins, Leo and Cleo, were mingling with everyone, and what handsome kids they were, another tick in the box for Dimple.

Sherry saw Dimple drift off to a corner with Bunny. She knew that she must join them soon, but her priority was to catch Dr Danny. Her attempt was hampered by Pearl, who seemed to appear out of the blue.

"Sweetie, shall we get a drink?"

"I couldn't right now, but in a wee bit I'll definitely join you, darling."

Sherry wasn't sure if Pearl was just a bit tipsy. Odd for her to be drinking more than usual.

Extricating herself gently from Pearl's clutches, she made a beeline to where the doctor was sitting. Sinking into the soft sofa next to him, she quickly picked up a mini curry puff and gave him a bright smile. They knew each other quite well as they moved in the same social circles.

She decided to get straight to the point.

"Danny, I heard you were the one that did the report on AJ's death."

"Yes, I was, Sherry," he mumbled through a mouthful of cheese aigrette.

"So, was it really a heart attack?"

"Well, truth be told, I don't know, but don't quote me," he grinned at her.

Honestly, thought Sherry. Nevertheless, she ploughed on.

"But, do you think it was definitely natural causes?" She winced as she said the words. She didn't want Danny to think she was a nutter. Thank goodness Zareen wasn't near enough to hear all this.

He looked at her while popping another cheese aigrette into his mouth, and once again replied with a mouthful of food.

"Well, I was told they had to move him from the mess of the soup, so they laid him on the bed." Gulping, he continued, "That's where he was when I arrived."

He grinned at her again. "He hasn't answered my question," she thought, and wondered whether he also had had one too many. Anyway, I best get all that I can out of him when it's still fresh in his head, she decided.

"I was just wondering if there had been some kind of foul play?" Her voice was a little weak, she knew it didn't sound too realistic and, frankly, seeing him looking so relaxed made her wonder if she really was quite bonkers.

Maybe Zee Zee was right. Maybe, after all, it was all in her head.

Leaning towards her, he peered at her with his large and slightly goggly eyes as if she were an interesting specimen, then proceeded to reply with an even wider grin, "You see, Sherry my dear, this AJ chap, who mind you, I had never met in the flesh…" He started laughing. Sherry ignored his chuckles hoping that he would get on with it. "… was quite chubby, didn't look very healthy to me at all. Short of doing an autopsy, one can only hazard a guess that it was either his heart or maybe an aneurism. We checked up with his GP in the U.K. who said that, apart from coming in with the odd flu, he never had any problems, but they did say that, unlike us in this glorious country, where we can walk into any hospital and get a treadmill test done, self-prescribed…" He now laughed out uproariously.

Sherry held her patience.

"… the doctors there don't suggest any of these tests unless there's a perceived problem, and there wasn't in his case. However, as we in the medical world know, an overall look at the patient can tell you a lot about his lifestyle and this AJ fella looked like he hadn't jogged or lifted a weight in the last twenty years, so, Sherry, my darling…" At this point he started laughing uncontrollably.

Yes, yes. I know my name is 'Sherry Darling', she thought with exasperation.

"… it was definitely a case of 'either/or'."

He grinned at her. "Are those curry puffs very spicy? You see, I have a sensitive tummy."

Either a heart attack or an aneurysm was what he meant, she realised, before being startled by a rather drunken slurred voice from behind the sofa. Leering at Danny and placing the tip of her finger on the tip of his nose, an extremely intoxicated Pearl giggled out the words, "EITHER you get yourself another drink, OR I can get yooooou one..."

Chapter Twelve

Aspirations

Sherry was a 'pure' Anglo Indian and it was with this frame of mind that she surveyed the scene in front of her.

She held her head ever so slightly higher than one would normally need to as she smiled gratefully to herself, thinking rather snootily, thank God I don't live on the plains. She shuddered at the thought of her last trip down the mountains to the vast flatlands of south India to visit relatives in the historical city of Madurai.

What a stay it had been. Hot and so very dusty, she couldn't even cross the roads without finding her eyes and nose clogged up with thick dust conjured up and then blasted through the air by the abundance of vehicles jostling for road space. It was so uncomfortable that on day two of her visit, she stopped wearing her lipstick because of the dust sticking to it! Yuk, she shuddered again at the thought of her 'no lipstick' so-called 'holiday'!

She was proud that Ooty was where she had always lived, a town filled with fresh, lush greenery. The views, wherever one looked, were invariably of gently rounded mountains and hillocks. Gentle, because little did people know that the Western Ghats were a whopping one hundred million years older than the famous Himalayas, thus wind, rain and all the other natural elements had had millennia to polish and round off tips and jagged edges.

Admiring the sights around her, Sherry proudly lifted her chin even higher. I had better get going, she thought. She was meeting Zareen at Mary's for an early drink that evening and had bought Mary's favourite cappuccino and lavender macarons from Pearl's Tea Room. As she made her way up the lane leading to Nun's Cross, Mary's home, she wondered where the 'Nun' bit came from, for, as far as she could remember, that property was always a monastery, or a sanatorium, or maybe it was a seminary. Yes, that was it, a seminary, named The Hermitage. It was positively teeming with priests, certainly there was never a nun in sight. Strange, the way things turn out. Maybe it had originally been an abbey. After all, her earliest memories of the seminary were of adult chitter-chatter on how very old the institution was. It could well have started out as an abbey.

She frowned as she remembered the piggery the priests had. They produced the most fantastic hams and sausages but the poor piggies, of course, were butchered for the meat. She had a sudden flashback of peering through the slats of the wooden-fenced pen they were in, cute, pink, and oinking away. Poor things.

Then there was Father Machado, a lovely, kindly man. He was the ultimate personification of the classic Catholic priest from 'those days', although Sherry's memories of him were from the eighties. He was tall and thin with a longish gaunt face, and, of course, was always dressed in a plain brown cassock.

He used to come to their school to advise the staff on the school's vegetable garden. Gardening was one of his passions. He was very stern with the staff on all matters concerning the need for gardening discipline, causing the staff to be rather rude about the dedicated and diligent man. 'Much-Ado Machado is coming this afternoon', they would warn each other.

With these pleasant memories still fresh in her mind, Sherry finally arrived at The Hermitage; the front door had a carved wooden sign hanging on it, proudly proclaiming, 'Nun's Cross'.

Comfortably seated in Mary's sitting room, Sherry said, "I'm not really sure about her."

"Why not, Sherry?" was the combined retort from both Mary and Zareen.

"Well, I remember when Violet was a teenager, she was quite odd… always running after boys that were a few years younger than her. It's almost as if, having no self-confidence, she felt better off with younger boys. I'm just saying that, after all these years, I don't think she's really any better off with her confidence level than when she was younger."

"Well, she's now married to a right buffoon, which must make her really question herself, and make her feel even more miserable, I'm sure," said Mary, and added cattily, "I know for sure she's a liar."

"Noooooo… really?"

"Yes, one of those habitual ones, you know, lies for no rhyme or reason. It's a habit with her."

"There's a reason as to why people become like this. It's always some kind of trauma they went through," Zareen said with absolute surety, looking terribly pleased with herself.

Sherry and Mary gave her a look, both being quite unimpressed with her theory. These medical people were all the same, an excuse for every flaw in one's character.

"Anyway, let's get back to where we were. I went through all AJ's papers that I brought back from the club and, honestly, there wasn't much. Of course, the only thing I was looking for was something that would indicate why someone would want to kill him, but I'm now having doubts," said Sherry, glancing at Zareen as she thought, maybe I should give it up.

Zareen took a sip of her drink and said, "Sherry, I know I've said this before and I'm saying it AGAIN. We're likely never going to know if anything untoward had taken place. We know so many people ourselves who have just dropped dead, so my recommendation is just leave it be, Sherry."

They went on to chat about the ball, excitedly. It was just a couple of days away.

"I'm far too old for these big parties," said Mary. Before protests could be sounded, she quickly clarified, saying, "Of course, I'll buy a ticket and, of course, I'll go, but I shan't stay too long. It's really a bit too glitzy and a tad la-di-da for plain old me, but I mean to support this town and, more importantly, the club. You know, girls, ever since 1979, I have had almost every single lunch and dinner there, whenever I have been in town."

This was a well-known fact amongst all of Mary's friends and acquaintances, but as is so often the case with older people, they love regaling and, frequently repeating, the humdrum details of their lives.

Having made her point, Mary rang the bell for Liza, her long-time maid.

It took some time for Liza to appear but when she did, her customary, dazzling smile made up for the delay.

"Ma?" Liza directed her gaze at Mary.

"Liza, Lady Fussington will be arriving soon. Please make sure you answer the doorbell promptly when she arrives."

"Yes, Ma," said Liza; giving the ladies another dazzling smile, she retreated.

Zareen sighed, "Thank God for our Nilgiris maids and butlers, but more so, thank God we can afford to **have** a maid."

"Yes, I agree, but I very much doubt the younger set will be able to afford them once they are running households. Definitely not with the huge hikes in salaries we're seeing every two, three years now," said Sherry.

Indeed, out of all the places in the enormous country that is India, it was, unexpectedly, in this hill station in south India, that one could still find domestics that were a far cut above all the others in the land. Most of them were descended from butlers, housekeepers, nannies, and maids who were the first generation that were trained directly by the British on the innumerable subtleties in various areas of domestic service. This training was passed down diligently and although now somewhat diluted, many still retained much of the mannerisms that were so pleasurable in the running of a household, albeit pleasurable to those employers who appreciated the old ways. Many these days either couldn't be bothered or outright rejected India's history with the British. "Just think how convenient it is that your Liza is our Philo's sister. We're always passing things through them to each other's homes!"

"Yes, soooo convenient, and did you know that the club boy, Chinnaswamy, is their nephew? Son of another sister of theirs. You'll remember her as the sister who died in that awful double cyclone during that November monsoon. He comes here often as we're just across from the club. It's such a pity he isn't all there, but at least he is able to hold onto his job at the club. In fact, he was here when you arrived, Sherry. He'd brought along his new bestie, a youngster like him. I think that for the first time in his life he has someone who looks up to him and he's really enjoying the adoration!"

Sherry piped up, "Oh, I know the boy you're talking about. I mean I haven't met him, but I saw him being trained at the club the other day. I actually thought he was Chinnaswamy. These boys all have the same haircuts!"

"Sorry to change the subject, Mary, have you ever used the Pest Control company? Sherry and I think we are about to have an ant invasion, of all things. We've never used professionals before though, so was wondering," said Zareen.

"No, never used them, but do you also have a rat problem? I don't mean inside your home, of course, but in the garden?" asked Mary.

"We certainly do, in the garden, but there's nothing one can do about it," replied Zareen with great conviction.

Mary shivered. "I can't stand having them, even outside. I've strictly told Liza this evening that she's to put out rat poison and get rid of them. They give me the creeps, and those two boys were all goggle-eyed about my instructions, honestly, but Liza understood it all perfectly." She finished her declaration with a superior sounding grunt.

Neither Sherry nor Zareen wanted to tell Mary that it just wasn't possible to get rid of outdoor rodents.

The room fell silent for a moment. Comfortable in their soft armchairs and pleased with their lot in life, the ladies looked at each other appreciatively.

Mary broke the silence; pouring them all another shot of sherry, she said, in a rather secretive tone, "I have something to tell you."

Two pairs of eyes were now firmly fixed on her.

"There's a very strong likelihood that I may be appointed onto the club committee, as of course, the first ever lady committee member."

The two pairs of eyes widened. "Goodness, Mary, what an honour!"

"It's not confirmed yet, girls, so keep it quiet. You never know with those men and what they will finally decide."

Chapter Thirteen

A, B, C & D

The rain from the previous night created a soft, early morning mist which was now rising rapidly from the ground and mixing with the rays of the sun. The garden, the drive, the trees, in fact everything in sight, was bathed in an ethereal light. It was a typical Nilgiri summer morning.

Ali Rasheed looked around. Everything was falling into place well and, having recovered from the to-do of the previous two weeks, he was finally starting to feel his old self again. Time really does heal! For a man who was fairly rigid in his daily routine, getting back to the normal daily problems of running a club was simply nirvana. Shifting slightly in his suit jacket, Ali was thrilled to get into the thick of it. After all, the Equestrian Ball was the single largest event of the year. The big three were soon arriving for their last look around. All the service details had been sorted out with Sherry and Anna. This morning Sherry, Bunny, and Dimple were popping in for a quick 'look see' before the party tonight. Although he was more than capable of ensuring everything was in place, Ali knew that women were what they were. They absolutely must double check every detail for themselves. Tedious, but there it was.

Bartholomew appeared from nowhere.

"Sir, Chinnaswamy says there's not enough firewood for tonight."

"Firewood? Did you say firewood?"

For a moment Ali went blank. He stared out into space, oblivious of the man in front of him. Eventually he snapped out of his mini trance to say, "There must be. I placed the order weeks ago..." Ali's voice trailed off. He now wondered, with some alarm, if he may have forgotten in the aftermath of the AJ problems.

"Leave it to me, Bartholomew."

Simple-minded waiters though they were, both Bartholomew and Daniel were his de facto assistants when it came to the practical side of running the club.

Bartholomew was glad to leave this problem on his boss's desk. Making his way to the staff room, he found Daniel in the enormous dining room, counting out the cutlery and making detailed notes in his diary.

"De-ni-al, let's have some tea before our break time is over."

Catching Chinnaswamy on the way, the three settled down to their break.

Taking a gulp of his hot tea, Chinnaswamy grinned at them and abruptly announced, "I think Jothi likes me."

The two older men looked at each other, then back at Chinnaswamy.

"Who said?"

"I'm saying, aren't I?"

"Be careful. You know what happened last time?"

"What happened last time?"

"You know, you tried to kiss that silly Rani girl and she shoved you down onto the wood pile. You cut your back so badly that you had to be on leave for two weeks and you didn't get paid. Then you got the flu and, again, you couldn't come to work for ten days and, again, you didn't get paid!" huffed Bartholomew, looking very exasperated. How could the dim-witted boy not remember all this, it was barely three months ago! He knew, though, that the deficient boy often recalled joyous childhood memories with singular clarity. Sighing, he realised that everyone must cope with some affliction or the other.

Daniel added to this mini tirade, "And what a lot of trouble it was for Mr Rasheed. You ended up in the hospital then the police got involved and then Mr Rasheed had to make sure they didn't find out about you being pushed by that girl. God knows WHAT WOULD HAVE HAPPENED if that came out! You might have been taken in by the police… and an investigation would have started, which would end up in God knows what all trouble for who all."

Chinnaswamy chewed on this, seemingly seriously, for some time. Bartholomew and Daniel could almost see the slow wheels in his head turning. He was certainly recalling the recent past, but being slow-witted, it was a challenge. His recall was quite sketchy.

Bartholomew added, "Now, you better be careful about that new boy, Siva. You're going everywhere with him, and I don't want him learning bad habits from you and getting into trouble. I have to train that boy up pukka and I don't want him daydreaming. Do you understand, boy?"

"Bartho-lo-miu, we better get back or else nothing will get done in time," urged Daniel.

Getting up, both men gave the youngster a warning look. "Be careful. Mr Rasheed is already fed up with you."

Despite this telling off, Chinnaswamy gave them another wide grin before slinking off to sort out what little was left of the firewood.

Bartholomew was still tired. The trauma of finding that horrible man with his chin in his soup would probably haunt him for the next few years, or maybe even until he went to his grave. He trembled at the thought of it all. He winced at what he knew was his very unmanly reaction to the death.

The trouble was he couldn't bring himself to tell anyone his first thought when he found AJ Panniker.

Poor Bartholomew had been, in the first place, absolutely terrified of AJ Panniker. He had been shouted at and mocked ruthlessly for the slightest perceived mistake while serving him his meals. He was ridiculed so much so that every time he was sent to AJ's room, or to his table in the dining room, Bartholomew was a bundle of nerves, ensuring that he would fumble yet again. So, on that dreadful night, when he knocked and entered at the precise time AJ Panniker told him to return for the trolley, and saw him, eyes wide open staring at him and the mess all around and the food on the carpet, Bartholomew didn't for a minute think he had died. He thought it was a cruel joke by Mr AJP, a joke to say, 'look at the mess you have to clear up now, you bloody fool!'

Bartholomew was so scared of what he saw that even thinking about it now made his chest hurt.

He thought back to when he set the tray that fateful night. Making sure that it was absolutely perfect. He remembered staring at the trolley and the curls of butter neatly laid in the tiny silver dish. Butter knife next to it, a butter knife and a soup spoon, neither would likely kill him if used as a weapon by AJ Panniker.

He remembered Chinnaswamy bringing in bags of firewood that night and hauling the bags past the neatly set room service trolleys. Where would we all be without this corridor? We could never be so efficient if it hadn't been built. Shaking his head in disbelief, he wondered about the architects of the club, whoever were they? How clever they were. Without this corridor, he would be half dead by now, having to make his way right around to the front of the club building for most of his daily jobs.

This 'life saving' passage had a door leading into the dining room. It was so much easier to get the firewood in rather than lugging it all through the kitchen. He remembered his younger days when he did Chinnaswamy's job. How agile he was, and... yes, strong, so strong. He could carry bags and bags of firewood, no shoulder pain, no neck pain... no chest pains. The doors going into the 'Gents' and 'Ladies' were back doors, so that the bathrooms could be cleaned discreetly. Go in from the passage with the equipment, clean and leave. No need to traipse through 'member areas', like they do in lesser clubs. The best of all the doors, the single most useful one, was the one door taking us to the guest rooms in seconds.

God knows how long it would take to get the food to the rooms if I had to push the trolleys out of the kitchen and go right around to the main hall and then to the guest rooms, he thought. Imagine what scoldings I would have got from Mr AJ with the food arriving cold. No, no, must forget that night. He rubbed his painful chest as he thought of the guests at the Queen's Bar that night. He knew that they were more aghast at his performance than they were at the dead body. When will I ever get my reputation back?

He brushed aside his regrets and went back to delightful thoughts of his corridor.

Chapter Fourteen

Francis, Phyllis and Mary

Francis

The gates were opened with panache and a 'salaam'. Francis gratefully drove through, past the enormous garden beds filled with artichoke plants, down the short drive, and stopped at his front door. Climbing out of the car, he gave the boy a thankful nod. The one thing Francis hated was having to stop his car, get out, open the gates, drive through, stop again, get out again, and close the gates. Yet he knew this was, after all, the Indian countryside, where such contraptions as gates were never going to work properly with a remote control. He chuckled, as he imagined what a hilarious sight it would be to watch Mary grappling with the remote control, the car, her shopping, and her handbag!

The long anticipated Equestrian Ball was tonight, and he was looking forward to it. He was yet to ask his sisters if any of them wanted a lift to the club. If there was one thing Francis was passionate about, it was stemming the terrible waste caused by today's lifestyle. He winced as he recalled a lunch party the previous year at a friend's home. They were celebrating their daughter's wedding anniversary. There were eight family members attending and unbelievably each one of them, including the couple, arrived separately, each driving their own car. No one in India seemed to care about their carbon footprint, but he was determined to fly the Fonseca flag high when it came down to this subject.

He had, of course, already offered to take Mary, but as she was just 'showing her face', she had hired a car for the evening, adding to the carbon footprint. He sighed at the thought of it.

Stepping onto his porch, he glanced up at the old Shiro plum tree. He had named it 'the one-plum wonder' for that was all they had got from it for the past two years. Now it was full of flowers, at, of course, the wrong time of the year. He knew it would not fruit as the monsoon rain and wind would start in a few weeks.

Unlocking the front door, he frowned slightly as he wistfully thought back to his younger days in Chater Hall. Although not handsome in the traditional sense, Francis had trustworthy eyes and a kind smile, making him a great favourite with the girls. He had looked forward to a life on his family's property, a pretty wife and a couple of kids running around. But it never happened for him; none of his relationships panned out, oddly. And so, here he now was. It wasn't that he was uncomfortable at the Hermitage, but he did have to put up with Mary's yappy little dogs always snapping at his ankles. If they still had Chater Hall, he would have had his own free-standing cottage by now, custom designed with lots of large windows. Bloody hell, was he going to be stuck in this place for the rest of his life?

Phyllis

As was her habit, Phyllis was sashaying in front of the full-length mirror, but she was unusually oblivious to her beauty. She didn't know what was bothering her though. She just couldn't get into the mood for the ball. Was it because this was the first time she was going to be at the club since the night of AJ's death, she wondered? But it couldn't be. She had certainly been more excited than upset when the discovery was made.

She tried to shake herself out of it but there was something definitely nagging her. It was a dark and heavy feeling. She thought back to that night. She was walking out of the card room just as AJ was walking into the main hall. The hall was empty as everyone was either at the Queen's Bar or was dining. She stood still in the card room doorway, watching him as he strolled casually up to the newspaper rack. He was browsing, deciding which paper he would take back to his room for his evening read.

Watching his nonchalant attitude, she was suddenly taken back to so many years ago. What a sad and sorry scene it was. Papa was sitting on the very edge of an armchair, almost falling off it, tears welling up in his eyes. It was the first time she had ever seen a man about to cry. It tore her heart. He was such a soft-hearted man, always spoke gently and kindly to his children, even when they deserved a good whack. It was at that exact point in time that the clever Phyllis Fonseca realised that their lives would spiral out of control.

Wincing, she shook herself again. She remembered how she wanted to walk up to AJ, take off one of her high heeled shoes, and hit him hard from behind, right on the back of his neck with the point of the heel cutting into his skin, but then she decided against it because he ought to be killed, not just thumped. Killed for the sake of Mama and Papa. Never mind her and Francis and Violet. They could manage the rest of their lives. It was thanks to AJ's father that Mama had completely collapsed, and Papa was an entirely crushed man. They were broken into bits, and AJ was now behaving as cruelly as his father.

Phyllis stood for a moment more. Yes, that was it. If he died then she would be fine because she knew that she couldn't live in the same small town as the man whose family so cruelly ruined her parents' lives and by his actions and had marred hers and Violet's and Francis' lives forever.

She turned around and walked back into the card room. It was empty; she sat down and thought about her darling Mama and Papa. At least they weren't in this miserable world any more.

Mary

Mary was highly excited about the ball, despite her declarations that it 'wasn't her kind of thing'.

"Liza, I want to see only the red saris."

Liza dutifully selected all the reds, maroons, and for good measure, the pinks. One never knew which colour might take Madam's fancy!

Mary leaned back in her armchair and, with a 'touch of the royal' about her, surveyed the glorious scene on the bed in front of her.

Each sari had its own story. Some were inherited, some were gifts to her from dear friends, and some bought by Mary for special occasions. She clearly remembered the arrival of each one of them. She wondered whom she would eventually leave this collection to. She had two nieces, both now living in Australia. Would they actually ever wear them, she wondered. There was her cousin's daughter, Sheena, living in New Delhi. Quite a highflyer she was, but a nice girl. Mary actually preferred her to the two Australians. Yes, when the time comes, she may leave the bulk to Sheena and a couple of the heirloom saris to each niece. After all, it was their right.

After much humming and hawing, and proving Liza's intimate knowledge of her employer, Mary decided on a dark pink sari with a hand-embroidered border.

Much of Mary's excitement was not so much the ball but the soon-to-be announced list of members who were to be appointed to the exalted club committee. Goodness knew this ultimate accolade did not simply plop itself onto Mary's lap. For the better part of almost two years, Mary had lobbied and persuaded and, in some cases, cajoled the men who were long-standing board members to 'loosen up a bit', move with the times and allow a lady member to be on the committee, if for no other reason than to be seen as the pioneering forward-thinkers that they were.

She smiled at her success. Yes, let them think it was their idea. Who cared really, as long as this feather in her cap became a reality? At just seventy-five, Mary was a sharp and active woman. There was so much she could contribute. She was familiar with the 'ways' of the club, the woes of female members, and she knew EXACTLY what was needed to make vast improvements to the dismal housekeeping practices, something which the all-male committee did not understand a thing about. After all, she was the oldest female member of the club and was the only club member, irrespective of gender, to visit the club TWICE every single day, and, goodness, what she had noticed behind the scenes was enough to raise many an eyebrow! All these transgressions had to be set right.

Chapter Fifteen

The Ball Is On!

Chinnaswamy was sitting on his haunches outside the kitchen, staring at the never-ending stream of cars steadily moving down the rose-lined driveway leading to the club car park. The headlights were blinding. His large round eyes blinked back tears, tears that came both from the sharp lights and from his sadness. It wasn't that he knew he would never own a car. That was something he'd never dare dream of. No, it was the rose bushes that were lit up by the headlights that made him think of his mum, Clara. She had worked in the club right up to her death.

Chinnaswamy shivered and blinked repeatedly. Flashbacks kept popping up in front of him, of a bright, sunlit drive, giant cream, peach, and yellow roses in full bloom on both sides of the driveway, of him skipping down the driveway ahead of his mum, her laughter as she tried holding him back... sitting with her during her breaks and devouring biscuits so generously given to him by the kitchen staff. He must have only been about twelve years old and how wonderfully warm and safe he felt, basking in her love. He yearned and yearned to be hugged by her again.

After she died, he had his two aunts to care for him. They were kindly, but it just wasn't the same. He closed his eyes now, squeezing memories from the back of his mind. Holding his legs up to his chest, he swayed slightly from side to side as he remembered her cooking in the kitchen, chatting with her as he got into his cosy bed. Swaying more now, he could actually smell the talcum powder she so generously sprinkled on herself every morning.

"Oy, mister... come oooooon," a voice boomed above his head.

A startled Chinnaswamy was brought back to reality by Daniel.

"Come on, hurry up. The last load of firewood came hours ago, and the dining room fireplaces haven't been stocked yet!" Chinnaswamy got up to load yet another fireplace with wood. He was happy now as he shook off his melancholy, knowing that after this, he was done for the night. He just hoped no one was going to rope him in as an extra hand in the kitchen!

The enormous front hall of the country club had filled quickly and was positively heaving after only an hour into the ball. Obviously, everyone wanted to get the most out of what they had paid for their prestigious tickets.

The ladies were swanning around in stunning evening wear, worn with the most gorgeous pieces of jewellery, some of which, as is quite the norm in India, were quite ostentatious. The men were in sharp suits, dinner jackets, or uniform.

Quite a lot of uniforms actually, if one took the time to notice. And why wouldn't there be? After all, housed just thirty minutes away, in the picturesque cantonment town of Wellington, was the oldest regiment in the Indian army, the legendary Madras Regiment, as well as the College for the Defence Services Officers, all in all, resulting in quite a substantial presence of smart and sharp officers.

Finishing a chat with one such officer, Arun turned to steal a glance at Violet. Something strange about her this evening. In fact, she had been like this for the last two days. She was excited and nervous AND giggly. If there was one thing you could be sure about Violet, it was that she was never ever giggly. He knew it had nothing to do with being at this glorious shindig. She was huddled in a corner, knocking back her gin and talking at the top of her voice to Mary and Dimple.

Well, what's good for the goose is good for the gander, he thought. As he turned around to head for the bar, he smashed into Bunny Fussington, causing her drink to spill onto his jacket.

"Arun dear, I can't get over the colours I'm looking at here tonight!"

As a way of a reply, Arun looked around him; there was happiness and laughter, and an awful lot of drinking and clinking going on. Glitz was everywhere to be seen. Oh well, if it takes care of the horses, then well and good. But before he could say a word in reply, Bunny continued.

"Arun dear, if there's one thing I can never understand, and I'm sure you'll agree with me here, is all these countries that have bright sunshine and blue skies, well they have houses and buildings all painted in beautiful whites and happy colours like yellows and blues and so on, and everyone dresses in gorgeous colours. I mean, just look

110

around. Whereas, for example, where I'm from, the sky is grey for most of the year. Hardly any sun you know, all the buildings are brown or grey and everyone dresses in blacks and greys and all these other depressing colours. I just don't understand, do you, dear?"

With her double chin wobbling, she looked at him with great expectation. Arun knew he had to escape but being fond of Bunny, he decided some small talk before dashing off would be in order. Thankfully, they were joined by Miki.

Miki, as the ever-gracious man he was, dutifully topped up their drinks and started telling them that dinner should be served in the next hour, after which the live band was going to start playing all the hits from 1965. Of course, Bunny and Arun knew this, but really, what else was there to chat about in such an enormous gathering, other than inane generalities? Certainly, one couldn't sit and have a decent meaningful conversation with the racket going on in the background.

Arun stole another glance at Violet, but she had drifted off. So had Mary, for that matter. Violet and Mary were now replaced by the General and his extremely anorexic-looking wife. A distracted-looking Dimple was offering them a bowl of crisps. Poor thing. Looks like she needs rescuing, he thought vaguely. He had, in fact, more important thoughts on his mind. Looking at his watch, he knew that she was probably waiting outside.

Dimple's head was hurting. Had the music got louder? Where are the children, she wondered? Cleo, no doubt, was huddled somewhere with Adam. Kiki and Koko were nowhere in sight, but Leo, thank God, could be seen at the other end of the room with a group of his friends.

Catching his mum's frantic wave, he went over to her. "Darling, can you find Mr Rasheed? He's nowhere to be found. I've got a dreadful headache coming on. Just find out if everything is on time for dinner and let me know, baba."

Leo sauntered off with his pal, Sam.

Dimple wasn't actually worried about the food. She knew it had arrived ages ago in the van boldly emblazoned with, 'Scrumptiousness from the Screwallahs'. Anna and Aidan were thoroughly reliable despite their thoroughly unreliable company slogan.

It was the club kitchen staff she didn't trust. From past experience, they were always 'all over the place' and invariably delaying the food service.

Her head was throbbing now. She wondered what had set it off. Her diamond encrusted watch told her it was already eight-fifty. Although it was an enormous hall, it was getting really warm now. Taking a much-needed sip of her icy Krug, she wondered if next year, she would plan it such that the dinner was served at eight sharp! The trouble with us Indians, she thought, is that for the life of us, we just can't get a party off the ground properly before nine. Even if you gave them a time of seven, guests would still arrive way past eight and look quite nonchalant about it.

Sherry and Bunny couldn't be found anywhere either, but she wasn't worried. She knew for sure they would have ironed out any wrinkles quite early on in the evening.

Mary appeared out of the blue. "Dear girl, can we do something about the heat in here? I feel almost faint."

Dimple agreed. The heat was probably why her head was throbbing so much.

"Dinner should be on in a minute, Mary, and it's much cooler in the dining room anyway."

"No, no, don't worry about me. I'm leaving now. Remember I'd said I couldn't manage a very long evening?"

"Are you sure you can't stay on? You've paid for dinner after all."

"I know dear, but I can't pull along much longer in a crowd like this. It's tiring, you know." Dimple knew just what she meant. Mary looked tired. It was the blasted stuffiness in here, she thought.

Where was Leo? Everyone seemed to be disappearing. No doubt he had been distracted, as usual, on the way to finding the secretary. She felt as if her head was about to break.

Maybe if I go outside and sit in the cool breeze for a bit the pain will get better. Her comforting thoughts were suddenly stopped in their tracks, for, from what she could see, dinner was finally announced, or so she thought. There now seemed to be some kind of commotion at the dining room door, and Leo was in the middle of what looked like a fully-fledged altercation. Oh, my goodness, what is happening? Is Leo trying to prevent people from entering? The band had stopped playing. People looked confused and panicky... and someone started screaming from inside the dining room.

Chapter Sixteen

A Picture Paints a Thousand Words

In a valiant attempt to stop guests from entering, Leo had splayed his arms across the dining room doorway.

He looked frantically around for his father.

An anxious Miki was trying his best to get through the dense and excited crowd. His sharp eye saw Leo's friend inside the dining room. What exactly he was doing, he couldn't fathom. It looked like Sam was talking to someone who was sitting down.

As Miki made his way towards the dining room, the screaming stopped abruptly, as if a tap had been turned off.

Luckily for Leo, Brigadier Chacko turned up beside him, and after a whispered exchange with Leo, took charge in true military style.

"Sorry folks, there's been a mishap in the dining room, please get back to the party and we'll let you know when dinner is served." His genial tone seemed to calm everyone down instantly. The music started up and, in a blink, the guests were back to where they were just moments ago.

Sherry was aghast. This was a very bizarre incident, to say the least. She made her way to where Dimple was standing.

She noticed Francis was already next to her; both looked troubled.

The three of them knew this was no 'mishap', by any stretch of the imagination. They strained their necks towards the dining room, but the door was now firmly shut... and probably locked from the inside. Leo, the Brigadier, and Miki had disappeared from sight. There was no doubt as to where they were.

Sherry couldn't bear the suspense.

"Francis, I think it's best we take Dimple outside. Won't you feel better sitting in some cool air for a bit, Dimple?" she asked, turning to her.

Dimple nodded, still quite mute, no doubt from shock.

She knew something had happened.

The three of them went outside and sank gratefully into armchairs on the verandah, but as soon as their badly needed drinks arrived, Sherry made an excuse and dashed off into the night.

"What was that about?" asked Francis.

"That's just Sherry for you. For sure she's making her way to the back of the building to get into the dining room through the kitchen entrance; she just has to find out what is going on."

Dimple's tone had a touch of pride in it, almost as if she felt taken care of by Sherry's perceived action and in her typically thoughtful way, she gave Francis a thankful smile in appreciation for his company.

Sherry gingerly opened the kitchen door and peeped inside. Her eyes widened in surprise. There was dead silence and not a soul about. She walked into the warm kitchen and across the vast stone flooring, towards the door that led into the dining room. She winced at how loudly her heels clicked on the old stones.

She quietly opened the second door and slowly craned her neck into the dining room to see what on earth the earlier incident was all about.

Sherry didn't quite know for a moment what she was looking at, as the scene before her seemed to be a still life straight out of a painting. All the occupants in the room were absolutely stock still and silent.

The kitchen staff were all there, huddled in a corner, motionless, with just their eyes anxiously moving about the room. They were standing right in front of an enormous arrangement of lilies.

Thanks to her nerves, she momentarily disregarded the seriousness of the situation before her and, instead, cringed at how horribly their uniform colours clashed with the hues of the pink flowers. She made a firm note that next time they would have to have more whites and yellows. Her eyes wandered across to the other side of the dining room. A short distance away from the fireplace, a crumpled little body of a young man lay on its face. The body's head had congealed blood all over its left side which had dribbled onto the wooden floor, forming a small dry pool. The fireplace poker lay beside the body; dried blood covered the bottom half.

Sherry shrank back in horror, clutching her pearls.

This is our boy, Chinnaswamy, she realised with a choke.

Tears quickly welled up.

Sitting on a chair a little away from the body was Ali Rasheed; his head was down, his face buried in his hands.

From the corner of her eye, she could see someone who looked like Daniel sponging the face of someone lying on the floor on the far side of the room, moaning.

Standing some distance away were Miki, Leo, Sam, and the Brigadier.

Miki started talking and, with a start, Sherry realised that she had peeped in at the exact few seconds when they all just happened to be still and silent.

There was pandemonium in the room now. Everyone was talking at the same time; the kitchen staff were mumbling to each other and one of them was muffling a sob.

"Leo, make sure the door is properly bolted," instructed Miki.

"This is a bloody disaster. We can't serve dinner here. The body can't be moved," said the Brigadier.

"I'm sorry, sir..." A weak voice emerged from the chair.

"Come on now, Ali, this isn't your fault," Miki replied.

At this point, Sherry bravely stepped forward, firmly putting her deep despair aside, and said, "Let's serve dinner outside. It's far too warm indoors and the verandah has ample space."

"How are we going to move everything, Sherry?" asked Miki.

"I think we can, with the help of the staff, with Bunny and I supervising. Pearl must be around somewhere too."

Quick decisions were made. The Brigadier and Miki would deal with the police. Leo would stay inside the dining room to make sure nothing was touched, and Sam would stay with Ali, in his quarters, as Ali was suffering from shock. "Give him a shot of warm brandy, Sam. I don't care if he doesn't drink. Just get it down him as we'll need him when the police arrive."

The staff were sworn to utter secrecy until the end of the evening. A good sum was promised to each of them if they all managed to keep mum.

Money talks, or silences, no doubt about that, thought Miki despondently.

Chapter Seventeen

... From Gypsies to the Great and the Good...

Sundar sat up.

"Do you mean an actual murder up at the country club?"

"Yes, sir, and there are also a few hundred guests there right now for a party of some kind."

Sundar sank back into his chair. His mind was racing. This was his chance. The once in a lifetime chance that, if not grabbed, would slip through his fingers and likely never come again.

He was terribly excited. This could well be a defining chapter in his career, to now step into another world and stand tall in his capacity as the chief investigating officer, amongst all those posh people.

Sundar Raman, Superintendent of Police, was the highest-ranking police officer in The Nilgiris. With several deputy superintendents under him, he wielded enormous power in the district.

Twenty minutes later, en route to the club with two of his officers, Sundar's thoughts were of his grandfather, who had also been a senior government officer in The Nilgiris during the sixties. What stories he was told of Ooty town, its colourful residents, the pristine beauty surrounding him during his early morning walks, and especially of this historical club. His grandfather was the municipal commissioner of the district. His status was such that he mingled with high society, tea planters, senior military figures, and many of the expatriate Germans who lived in Ooty at that time, working on the Indo German agricultural project. His grandfather was often at this club. He had magical stories to tell the young boy sitting on his lap. The larger-than-life characters, the delicious food, the table service… it was all quite another world, and one the young boy never thought he would enter. Until now. Of course, the intelligent Sundar knew that this would only be a fleeting interlude in his career. He very much looked forward to meeting the club members and wondered if they would still be like his grandfather's friends. Doubtful. After all, that was fifty years ago.

He had felt very out of place since his arrival in Ooty five months ago. For a start, it was January and freezing cold. He had really suffered from the weather, more so as he had just been transferred from the bustling south Indian metropolis of Chennai, one of the world's largest cities. In Chennai, he dealt with all the crimes and criminals imaginable. The city had a thriving underworld and was rife with drug dealers, brothels, and everything else in between.

Eyeing the tall cypresses as the car sped on, Sundar thought of the stark turn his daily routine took after arriving here. The genteel town of Ooty was mostly filled with refined polite citizens. Most of the crime involved the odd con man or pick pocket. With a smile, he recalled his first week at the station when one of his officers made an important sounding announcement, "Sir, the Narikuravas have arrived."

The Narikuravas are the nomadic gypsies of Tamil Nadu. Sundar was, in fact, astounded to have recently learned that gypsies all over the world had their genetic roots in India. The Narikuravas arrive once a year in these mountains and stay for a few months, setting up campsites in the countryside, quite often in Ketti valley. The problem with them is that they have dogs, and the men venture out at dusk with these dogs on leashes on a determined mission of absolutely no good, mostly petty thieving and the like. The locals are afraid of them. The gypsy men are brazen in their bid to rifle homes, shops, and warehouses. Any guard or watchman present certainly didn't ruffle their feathers. Although it meant that now vigilance had to be stepped up, it was a far cry from the constant state of high alert that Sundar was so accustomed to.

The driveway up to the club was lit and he noticed the thickets of shola trees he had heard of from his grandfather. They had been asked to come around the back of the building as none of the guests dining outside on the porch knew about the murder.

As the car passed the front of the clubhouse, he could see beautiful people, dining and laughing as they chatted, seemingly with hardly a care in the world.

Chapter Eighteen

Suppositions

Buxey Lodge, pre-dawn

With a heavy heart, Sherry knocked on Zareen's door.

"Is that you, Sherry? Come in."

Sitting on the edge of her bed as Zareen propped up her pillow, they got down to the inevitable conversation.

"I can't begin to think how we're going to face Philo."

The time was just quarter to six and it was still dark outside, but the girls had decided to meet early to plan how they would break the frightful news of her nephew's brutal death to Philomena.

"She'll be totally broken and will either go off to spend time with Liza or will want Liza here for a few days. That's for sure."

"Poor boy. He was a sweet-natured lad, irritating at times but we knew nothing could be done about that. Who could have done such a thing, Sherry? And with such a lot of people milling about. It's as if we now have a madman in our midst…" Zareen trailed off, her tone full of disbelief.

"Philo will be coming up with our tea soon. I don't think we should be telling her as we're sipping it, very insensitive; maybe we should go down before she comes up."

Agreeing, Zareen got out of bed for a quick wash. Sherry went to the window and drew the curtain. Dawn was just breaking, and the tips of trees could just be seen against the sky, but she saw nothing as her mind was full of last night's events. The men had taken advantage of her spearheading the change of dinner venue and didn't let her back into the dining room when the police arrived. Johnny just shooed her away saying she was needed out front. She was bitterly disappointed. She couldn't figure it out but there was something about the little scrunched up body, with the poker that carelessly lay beside it. Not that she had ever seen a battered body before, so why couldn't she shake off this strange feeling? It was that poker, more than the body, she felt, so carelessly thrown on the floor. It gave her the distinct feeling that the killer had thrown it down with a haughty and satisfied shake of his, or her, head.

She felt tired and her eyes were hurting. She had hardly slept, of course. All through the short night, her mind was on poor Chinnaswamy. Who in this world would want to kill such an innocuous being?

She started. There was a knock on the bedroom door at the same time that Zareen came out of the bathroom.

In came Philo with Zareen's tea. Her arrival was a good thirty minutes earlier than usual and she looked as if she was about to make a statement, no doubt about Chinnaswamy. Before they could take in their utter surprise at the sight of their Philomena, standing there straight backed and looking fairly put together when they had expected to have to deal with a heap, Philomena said good morning, rather more crisply than usual and laid down her tray.

"Have you heard?" she asked, looking at them expectedly and sniffing. They noticed her eyes were red. That certainly wasn't quite the reaction they expected to get from her, but before they could absorb her astonishingly controlled behaviour, Philomena spoke again. In a high-pitched voice she said, "Chinna's best friend, that boy, Siva, has been murdered!" Oh my God, another murder! Thought Zareen. I was absolutely right; there really is a madman on the loose. Plopping down on her bed, she turned to look at Sherry, aghast at this news. Sherry was staring at Philomena. So, Siva has also been killed, but when and where? Since Philo hadn't yet said a word about Chinnaswamy, she realised that Philo appeared to be in shock. Completely and utterly.

"Philo, just sit down for a minute," she said, firmly, as she pulled the dressing stool forward.

Philomena sat and started talking about Siva again. Sherry wondered whether she had to be taken to a doctor.

The problem is that she's in so much shock that she's blocked out Chinnaswamy's death from her mind altogether. Unless, of course, she hasn't heard about it yet... oh no, what a mess this is. Sherry and Zareen couldn't believe their ears. Both boys, murdered.

They couldn't make out what exactly she was saying now as she had started to cry, but she did make one comment which sounded quite clear.

"... and he's so upset, he wants to know if he can come and stay for a few days. He says he's very scared."

"Who is scared?"

"Chinnaswamy."

Sherry sighed. In her gentlest tone, Sherry reminded the poor lady that Chinnaswamy was dead.

"No, ma'am, he's in the kitchen."

You mean, you wish he was in the kitchen, Sherry thought. Yes, we'll just have to give her something to calm her nerves and she should be all right.

Watsonia, eight a.m.

Violet was warming her hands with her coffee cup.

"It's definitely someone working in the club, and it could even be Ali, though I just hate the thought of it being him. If it was a club employee, who else could it be with the gumption needed for such a thing? The rest of them are so wishy-washy. Maybe the boy had seen something illegal going on and maybe, if Ali was involved, he realised the boy knew something. If Ali did do it, I can only think that he did it at that time, hoping that there won't be any suspicion on him because of the huge crowd there last night. And wasn't it him who 'found' the body? Don't they say that that's usually the murderer? I'm only guessing, mind you. It could of course be any one of us," finished Violet with a determined nod of her messy head.

"I just think there's something really weird going on. If he wanted to do him in, why inside the club? He could have coshed him on his head outside somewhere, like that remote firewood shack they have," said Phyllis.

Before Violet could answer, Geoffrey piped up. "Well, it depends, of course. We don't have a clue as to who did it but if you look at your Ali theory academically, maybe the lad was blackmailing him and gave him an ultimatum. Ali just couldn't bear it any more and, what with the tension of getting the ball off the ground, excuse the pun, he hit him then and there. It's definitely an unpremeditated murder. I'm sure that's what the police would say."

Taking another sip of his coffee, he added, "I say, Vi, can I add a dash of rum to this? Jolly good coffee, but I need a jolt thanks to the fiasco last night. Johnny called me in for a tête-à-tête before the police came, you know. Awful thing to have happened. He's quite upset. Doesn't know what to think."

"Did he have any ideas, Geoff?"

"No, no, we don't speculate on these things. This will have to be a rather large investigation given the enormous area of the club and all the people there, although we decided to make it very clear to the police that the entire kitchen and dining was really a 'no go' area for the guests. We can't have a few hundred of us being questioned anyway. The police won't get anything right and there'll be a lot of repetition. You know the sort of thing I mean, 'I arrived, I was at the main hall at the party, went to the Gents, or Ladies, as the case may be, a couple of times, otherwise stayed in the hall until we were called for dinner'. By which time, of course, we all know the poor kid was dead. No, no, this was an inside job, no doubt there. Nothing to do with us, either. Ali did it or one of the club staff did."

Violet looked up slowly from her coffee mug and thought, rather shrewdly, 'you're rather more pompous than I gave you credit for.'

The Kitchen, nine-fifteen a.m.

Anna was hysterical, to put it mildly.

"They're going to blame US, Aiden. US! Don't you GET IT? We were THERE! We were alone and that boy came in and out WHILE WE WERE THERE! Don't you UNDERSTAND ANYTHING?" she shrieked.

Aiden looked exhausted. All his balanced replies had been thoughtlessly thrown aside as she relentlessly banged on and on about how they were going to be blamed and end up in the gallows.

"How will the children manage, Aiden? HOW? We'll have left them NOTHING but this property, which is as good for nothing as it can possibly be."

"Get a hold of yourself, Anna. The police aren't stupid, and they'll need evidence."

Taking on a sarcastic tone, she continued, "You're the one who has to get it together, you don't want to see the reality of all this. WE AREN'T one of those posh club members, Aiden! UNDERSTAND! We can't get ourselves out of this mess because we don't know anyone in 'high places'. Neither can we buy ourselves out of this because we don't have a cent, and that's thanks to you, too!"

She sat down, exhausted.

Aiden could not for the life of him understand why he was being blamed. After all, it wasn't his fault they were in the empty room when the firewood boy was there but just when he thought she had finished her frantic tirade, she started up again.

"You know what the police are like. They can fix this on us JUST LIKE THAT, with a snap of their fingers, just so they can say they solved a case at the famous Ooty Country

Club. We're as good as dead ducks, Aiden!" she wailed, standing up again.

She should get to bed and jolly well stay there for two days, he decided.

Looking at the condition she was in, Aiden decided it was probably best that she stayed in this feverish state for a while longer. It will exhaust her, and she just, just, just may not remember that one small thing. Maybe I can sneak a sedative into her cocoa tonight, he thought, congratulating himself smugly.

Chapter Nineteen

Realisations

Buxey Lodge, nine-thirty a.m.

"So, it wasn't our fellow after all, and Philomena was absolutely right all along. I could have sworn it was him. If only they had let me in again, Zareen, I'd have realised." Sherry's voice was full of regret.

Firmly ensconced at their dining table, eating hot toast, and drinking strong coffee, Sherry and Zareen were grateful to be participating in such mundane activity.

Tiffany, lying under the table, let out a hopeful whimper but, sadly, only received a warning look in return. It wasn't likely that she would get any titbits from the table this morning. No one was in the mood to indulge her.

Sipping her coffee, Zareen said, "What idiots we must have seemed. We were, let's admit it, quite superior in our tone with Philo when we didn't believe her about Chinnaswamy sitting downstairs. We still can't actually say 'all's well that ends well' in this case because there's still a poor, dead boy lying in a morgue. Chinnaswamy is very upset, it seems. Siva admired him terribly and was probably the only person who's ever looked up to him, and naturally he's terrified. Look at the way Siva was battered, like some helpless little creature. I just can't imagine what state Ali must be in."

"Yes, he had to work so hard to get to this position in life and for this to happen so soon after AJ's death is enough to get anyone depressed."

"Do you remember his parents, Sherry?"

"Gosh, yes. His mum worked in the Beaconsfield estate, in their clinic. She wasn't quite a nurse but something like a senior nursing assistant, I think. She could be a bit odd, I guess these days they would call it OCD, but they didn't have a name for it when we were kids. If they did, the general population wasn't as familiar with the term as we all are now. Every time she saw a child, she was compelled to straighten out the child's dress, or collar, or tuck in a bit of shirt peeping out. All quite harmless but in this day and age, she'd probably be arrested for being a paedophile! His dad, coincidentally, worked at the Blue Mountain Pharmacy. The pharmacy was sold, and the new owner ran it into the ground. When it finally closed, Ali's dad lost his job. After that, he drifted from one pharmacy to the other. He was a hard worker but none of the new employers paid as well as Blue Mountain did, so life became even harder. They did have to scrape together through most of their life. Ali didn't have a carefree childhood by any stretch of the imagination."

Looking suitably despondent in response, Zareen changed the subject by asking what Sherry thought of Pearl's drunkenness at The Dawn a few nights ago.

"Not like her at all, was it, Zareen? In fact, she's not much of a drinker so I can't think why she got into that silly state. Maybe I should go see her in the next couple of days to have a cosy chat with her and pull her out of this funny mood." Sherry's voice trailed off; being reminded of that cocktail party reminded her of her chat with Dr Danny. Her thoughts now drifted back to AJ. The way they found him, in that strange and theatrical setting, and now an innocent young man has been brutally murdered, a few weeks later, in the same building. There's something here that I can't put my finger on... but, by hook or by crook, I damn well will. A smidgen of the 'Sherry spark' now returned. She took a comforting bite of her toast, noticing not the melting butter dripping off its edge.

The Ooty Country Club, nine-forty a.m.

Ali Rasheed was sitting up in bed. His pillows propped up such that his aching back was properly cushioned. He looked around his bedroom. The chintz curtains were partially drawn to let in the day. Two windows were opened, and the light breeze brought in exhilarating wafts of eucalyptus. He drew a deep breath, enjoying for a brief moment a semblance of his regular morning routine. He knew there were just a few days left for him to enjoy the simple pleasures of open windows and eucalyptus in the air, as the weather was turning quickly with the southwest monsoon setting in rapidly, and much earlier than usual.

He had decided that he wasn't getting out of bed for a few days.

He was completely drained. Anyway, the powers-that-be had decided to close the club for a few days until the dust had settled and the staff had recovered somewhat. Yes, there was absolutely no need to get out of bed. God knows he badly needed the rest.

His head was throbbing from the trauma of the murder and the relentless police questioning which went on and on into the night. Then there were the club staff. What an atrocious situation that was to deal with! Some of them were hysterical, some were totally numb. He was a very worried man. Neither Brigadier Chacko nor Mr Ponnappa had brought up the subject of the club member who started spreading those rumours about him illegally cutting trees and selling them off for firewood without the committee's approval. He didn't know if they hadn't brought it up on purpose or that they had plain forgotten about it, considering the stress they were under.

He shivered. These firewood boys had known all about the vile gossip that just came out of nowhere and pervaded his existence for months.

Trouble and death seemed to have seeped into his life these past few months. He didn't know who had started the rumours. He had wondered if it could have been Francis because for some odd reason Francis seemed very friendly the same week the ugly talk had erupted.

Then a few weeks later, an unexpected beast arrived, a black cloud from his teen years. AJ was so full of himself that he hadn't, for even a moment, remembered who Ali was. Ali, who he used to scoff at because he was so poor at sports. Then all the other kids started ganging up on him too; herd mentality had set in firmly. Ali shivered as he remembered 'the dark years' as he called them. He had begun to lose grades. He started to feel scared and depressed, and finally failed the end-of-the-year exams. He struggled with the two remaining years he had left of secondary school and only managed to get through by blocking AJ from his mind completely.

Then there was the stress of organising the ball straight after AJ's death whilst trying to calm the distraught staff.

Ali took in another deep breath, enjoying the scent of eucalyptus and deciding once and for all he was going to stay put for a few days. He knew he needed to think calmly. He had heard about the new S.P. and how well he had done on the sensational case of the film star stabbed to death in Chennai last year. He had apprehended the murderer in a matter of days. It was all over the national newspapers for weeks on end. What on earth would transpire now? What would he uncover, this new man now in charge?

Willowbund Police Station, eleven forty-five a.m.

S.P. Raman was standing at the window, looking out at endless fields of cabbages and potatoes. Mist was moving rapidly in from the west and the trees on the side of the fields were swaying with the strong wind. So, this was the start of the monsoon season that he had heard so much about. The winds would start howling at night, he was told, and the thick, constant mist would cause untold problems.

He brought himself back to the disturbing murder. The murder of a harmless young trainee waiter in such a prominent venue with such a large number of guests present spoke of nothing less than an urgent decision by the killer, a killer who knew him and who had decided to take the risk.

It meant the killer had no time to lose. Siva had to be killed immediately. Certainly, the better option of killing him in a lonely misty country lane was not an option. This could only mean that the victim was a blackmailer or had witnessed something he should not have. But what? What he saw of the guests last night left him with no doubt that if Siva had seen someone kissing or making out with someone they shouldn't have, no one would have been in the least bit bothered. No, it was something sinister, but again, what? The other train of thought he could investigate was that of a mad killer at the start of a rampage. He somehow doubted it, but one never knew. Maybe a guest? Very doubtful, as he was categorically told that the whole area was sealed off, except to the club employees and the caterers. Who, exactly, were these caterers? He knew that the details were recorded last night. I had best start with them as soon as I finish with the club staff. We don't want to give the staff enough time to come up with plausible stories for their whereabouts.

He sat at his desk thinking of his time at the club last night. He was met at the entrance by the club president and two of the senior club members. Their demeanour was very 'proper', in the old-fashioned sense. They were upright, calm, and clear on the facts. He believed them when they said nothing had been touched since the discovery, although that didn't speak for whatever could have been changed, or, for that matter, removed by the killer after the murder. Yes, vital evidence may have been removed. The poker revealed no clear fingerprints, only numerous smudgy indiscernible ones, which was a great pity.

They couldn't get much information from the club staff about the victim, Siva Ranjan. They were all too shocked and exhausted. The secretary had said that the boy had just joined three months ago and was a local chap, parents were tea pickers and lived more than an hour away on an estate. Siva didn't want to be a tea picker. He wanted some 'bright lights' in his life and came to town looking for a job where he could rise up the ranks. Poor poor chap, he thought. He remembered seeing his face at the morgue. A fine-boned face with thinnish lips and a well-shaped nose. Nice clear complexion too. Sundar had lost count of how many dead Sivas he had seen in his career.

He sat down. He had a strange, unsettled feeling. It was this new posting. He felt he had nothing anchoring him down. He had no roots here and his instincts told him that unless he started making a few contacts and hopefully a trusted friend or two, this case may well slip through his fingers. This was not a cut and dried 'drive-by bashing' by any stretch of the imagination, he concluded. This murder is part of a much bigger story.

Chapter Twenty

Nothing in Life Is Black and White

So, here was Pearl, three days after the ball, sitting with Sherry in the kitchen of her tea room on a Tuesday morning. They had the place to themselves as the staff would only get in after an hour.

They were oblivious to the view outside. The large windows looked out into a serene valley this morning, with soft sunshine in the east and mist sweeping down from the west. The valley looked almost as if two photographs of quite different seasons had been torn in half and roughly taped together.

Munching on a warm scone, Sherry was keen to plunge into the topic of Pearl's uncharacteristic and embarrassing behaviour at Dimple's party, but thought it diplomatic to first bring up the inevitable topic on everyone's mind at the moment, the bizarre and brazen murder of the club trainee waiter.

"Did you see him in the dining room while you were setting up your meringues? Apparently, the poor guy was in and out of the room like a jack-in-the-box."

Looking at Pearl, with eager anticipation, Sherry received only silence in return.

Having known her all her life, Sherry knew that something was up, and in any case with Pearl, it was invariably a situation of 'tread carefully'. Sherry knew both the murder and the cocktail party were delicate subjects and Pearl, being of a delicate nature, meant that Sherry had to now tread carefully!

To her surprise, Pearl started talking.

"Actually, to answer your question, I need to backtrack to Dimple's party."

Her deadpan tone and words were totally unexpected. Sherry, who was now halfway through her third scone, nodded encouragingly.

"I'm not sure if you remember the details that evening, Sherry. I, for one, can't remember the party all that well because apparently I was quite tipsy."

She looked at Sherry, embarrassed. Biting her lip, she continued. "Bunny phoned me the next morning. She asked me what the matter was as I had behaved in a most 'unladylike manner', her words. She wasn't nasty or anything. More inquisitive and trying to be helpful, if help was needed, I guess. I was so dismayed when Bunny told me I drank an awful lot and had to finally be taken home in Dimple's car. I prodded her for details as I was so aghast. She was a bit overwrought as I think she didn't want to upset me. It seems I was mostly teetering through the evening and ended up throwing myself at that out-of-shape, sloppy, Danny Zach, whom I barely know. I can't begin to tell you how much I wanted to just crawl into a hole after that phone call. Imagine what people must have thought, Sherry, 'the lithe and graceful Pearl Veeraswamy, owner of the well-established Pearl's Tea Room, was seen tipsy and looking downright ridiculous at a very posh party'. It was enough to make me want to vomit."

Taking a gulp of her hot lemon water, she continued, "After finishing the call with Bunny, I just couldn't bring myself to go to the Equestrian Ball and have all the same faces looking at me and remembering Dimple's cocktail party. Mind you, I had no intention of redeeming my expensive ticket. Why should the poor horses suffer because I royally messed up?"

Sherry nodded her agreement and gave her an understanding smile.

"So, that evening I drove up past the main clubhouse, right up to the back where the deliveries are made, and gave the twenty trays of meringues to Nava, the head chef. I didn't go inside at all and was never in the dining room, thank goodness."

Now that the night of the murder was mentioned, Sherry decided to get on with the real reason for her visit.

Convinced that Pearl's excessive drinking had something to do with AJ's reappearance, and convinced that something was not quite kosher with AJ's death, she felt she must grab every link to AJ that came her way, in order to come to some conclusion. As juicy as uncovering a murder might be, she was under no illusion that, if it was not a natural death, it may even have been an accidental death, with AJ having no one to blame except himself.

Sherry also had a sneaky feeling that Pearl had been listening in on her conversation with Dr Danny; so focused had Sherry been as to not miss a thing he was saying, with his mouth full of food, she had been oblivious to all else. But, in retrospect, she felt the real reason for Pearl's hovering was because she wanted to know what he had to say about AJ. It had nothing to do with being flirty. After all, she did say he was out of shape and sloppy, both very unattractive features in a man.

There could only be two reasons for her eavesdropping. Either it had to do with the fact that, as she said at the funeral, AJ was, after all, on the brink of becoming her brother-in-law, or that she knew something about his death… and that 'something' had to only remain with her.

Looking at Pearl in a new light now, she hesitated on how to move forward. A distant hum from a lawn mower added to the awkward quietness. Not wanting to create a maudlin atmosphere, she nevertheless brought up the subject of Avril, in the hope she would start talking about AJ.

"Imagine if Av had been alive and seen or heard of AJ's unexpected death. It would have been very hard on her. She really truly loved him." Her words had done the trick.

Pearl replied, "I know everyone thinks I hated AJ and that when he came back, I was reliving Avril's death all over again. The thing is, Sherry, and I know you'll now never look at me the same way again, no one, not even you, really knows what happened when Avril died."

Taking a sip of her water, Pearl continued. "The thing is, no one knows this, but AJ didn't abandon Avril when she was pregnant. Everyone thought he had because Avril let them think it. That was the type of person she was. Everything was always about her and her being in the limelight and being sympathised with. When Avril found out she was expecting, and although AJ wasn't exactly thrilled, he did say he would return. If you remember, he had to go to England and couldn't delay the trip because of his grandmother's death and all the paperwork that had to be sorted. She didn't want him to go. Avril absolutely convinced herself that if he stayed and saw the baby, then, if he still had to go to England, he would return but she was also absolutely certain that if he left before the baby was born, he would never come back."

Shifting in her chair and taking a deep breath, she continued. "And nine months is a long time to be hanging about, and honestly, she was barely a few weeks on."

Sherry merely nodded, not wanting to break the momentum.

Pearl continued, "Avril became utterly hysterical when she heard he had made up his mind to go to England immediately. What a palaver it all was! She began to wail and became all clingy, and then there was a big shouting match, and at that point she decided to 'show him', her words mind you, Sherry, her words."

Biting her lip again, she said, "I asked her what she meant, and she simply said, 'you'll see'. I was so fed up with her at that point, Sherry. I told her off. Told her she was being a silly, selfish cow and that she didn't know what a good thing she was onto with AJ but she was suddenly looking smug and calm and so I thought she had probably decided to let it all go. I was an idiot. I should have realised the smug look meant something was up. I think she thought, stupidly, that she could half hang herself and would be rescued, and that would make AJ think twice and stay. She went upstairs and I called AJ. I was even more stupid than Avril. I don't quite know what I was thinking or what I was planning to say to him. The thing is, Sherry, I was completely and totally infatuated with him and being so distraught with the unnecessary mess around me, thanks to her, I wanted to let him know, in some weird way, that I would always be there if it didn't work out with Avril."

Pearl suddenly burst out, sobbing, "There I was fumbling on the phone, trying to snare a man my own sister was madly in love with and pregnant, too. Oh God, Sherry, how could I have been so nasty, so cruel, so completely mad?"

Pearl started blowing her nose aggressively. Sherry sat stock still, still afraid she would stop the flow if she spoke.

Sniffing hard, she went on, more loudly than before, "There I was, talking rubbish on the phone. I don't think he could even hear me properly... and then something came over me. Did I come to my senses? I don't know, but I suddenly disconnected. I just sat there, trying to take it all in. What I had just done, I mean. After a few minutes I realised that the house was dead silent. Everything was so still. I started to get a strange, panicky feeling. You know what it was like with Avril. There was always noise about when she was around. At the very least, it would be music she had put on. That was the exact moment I knew something very bad had happened. I ran upstairs calling her name out all the way up... and you know the rest, Sherry," she finished in a bare whisper.

Sherry took a deep breath. So, dear, sweet Pearl was trying to snare her sister's fiancé while silly Avril was trying to create a scene upstairs hoping her sister would cut her down at the last minute, only her sister was otherwise occupied.

That was the sum of it. Sherry sighed.

Chapter Twenty-One

Plans

Glenealy House

Bunny was aimlessly fiddling with the ornaments on the dining room sideboard. Having just finished a ridiculously late breakfast, she was wondering if she should get a posse together to get the 4-1-1 on the murder that had shocked Ooty to the core.

Gosh, I've gone all 'American' on myself, she thought, but she knew why. With a rueful smile, she recalled what her life was like barely two years ago. This was the time of the year she and James made their ritual summer trip to New York. They would stay for the better part of summer, enjoying the company of old friends and all the city had to offer it's multitude of eager cultured visitors.

Sighing, she shook herself out of the wave of melancholy that overcame her. Change is part of the journey of life. I simply must buck up, she told herself.

Bunny had named her new home in India 'Glenealy House', after the main estate she and James lived in for most of the year. She had thought of bringing his ashes to India but instead decided to scatter them on the estate that he loved so much and had grown up on.

She would have been so thrilled to have had him sitting proudly on her bedroom mantelpiece. What on earth would James have thought of her being a few yards away from such a brutal murder. With another deep sigh, she cast her whimsical thoughts aside. One must move on!

Sitting down, she looked at the list of 'posse possibilities' on her mobile, Sherry topped her list. Sherry had actually seen the body! The whole scenario was quite unbelievable. She knew it was bad taste, especially for someone as evolved as she was, but she couldn't help the thrilling tingle she felt at the thought of the whole appalling matter!

Mary was also on the list, although Bunny heard she had left the ball quite early on. She knew Mary was a beady-eyed old thing and nothing much escaped her. Yup, she thought. Mary was a definite yes.

Dimple was a yes, too, especially with Miki having dealt with the police. She crossed out Pearl. After her last chat with the girl, she hardly thought she would cheerfully come over, put her feet up, and have a cosy gossip.

I should add a couple of men, she thought, but which of them is worth calling? Of the first two men that came to mind, Geoffrey was the voluble one. Francis was pretty closed mouth, but then… one was a Fonseca and the other was 'Fonseca attached'… which meant that Vi would probably hear all that would transpire at her little gathering.

Bunny sat back in her chair.

There's something not right about Violet these days and, goodness knows, she did seem very distracted at the ball. Bunny shook herself free of her thoughts. Distracted

143

or not, Violet wouldn't have seen anything amiss without saying so. Still…

Watsonia

Violet was throwing a sandwich together for her lunch, a big, meaty, roast beef sandwich with layers of lettuce she had just picked. The strips of meat kept flopping out and she roughly shoved them back in place.

She caught a glimpse of her reflection in the windows. The previously hesitant double chin had now definitely set in. She was fed up, sad, and angry. Nothing had panned out in her life. Just yesterday she was twenty. She was sparkly. She was also pretty and about to embark on a wonderful life with her brilliant husband. The world was truly their oyster. But now here she was, well into her fifties with nothing to show for the thirty years since. There was only one description for Arun, 'slimeball'. She blinked back tears of frustration as she realised she was nothing but a fool to have taken this long to face up to the fact that she had married a first-class creep… All she wanted to do now was to kick him in his face.

She hated him and she hated AJ. Both men were responsible for the two gaping black holes in her heart.

AJ is dead now. When and how will Arun go? Until he goes, I won't be whole again. Tears ran down her cheeks. Everyone took her to be a highly distracted woman, suffering from menopausal hysteria, but she knew exactly what he had done.

Chapter Twenty-Two

A.R. and S.R.

Ali was sitting in his office with the S.P.

His dream of a three-day rest in bed never happened thanks to the police turning up constantly, from the morning after the murder, asking about all sorts of odd things.

In true Indian style, and with great deference, Ali had offered the S.P. the chair behind his desk. However, in true un-Indian style the S.P. said he would be quite happy to sit in the visitor's chair, facing the secretary. The decline flustered Ali. He didn't like it when the balance of things was turned upside down. It unnerved him no end.

Disheartened and exhausted, Ali knew that he must, nevertheless, give a positive impression at this interview and steer the S.P. away from hearing that nasty gossip about the firewood. He couldn't have any suspicious eyes on him.

This was his first one-on-one interview with the newly appointed S.P., and if there's one thing he knew for sure, every new broom will sweep clean. This man will be no exception to the rule... and Ali was disinclined to be swept into a cell. With dark patches under his eyes, he looked at Sundar Raman with trepidation, wondering what his first question would be.

In return, Sundar appraised the man sitting before him. From what he had heard, Ali Rasheed was an upstanding man with a good record at this club. Why then did he look so ill and exhausted?

He knew from experience that people often reacted like this simply because the incident, crime, or murder was the last straw after a period of difficult or depressing situations. However, often enough, it was also an indication of plain guilt.

Leaning forward slightly, the S.P. spoke.

"So, let's go over this again. You yourself did not find the body. You sent…"

He looked down at his notes for reference.

"… a 'Bartholomew' to find the victim, Siva? Correct?"

"Yes, sir."

Sundar knew he had not yet seen Bartholomew as he had to be heavily sedated that night. Of course, the next day, he was in no condition to be questioned. However, it mattered not to Sundar. His well-honed instincts told him that the questioning of Bartholomew could wait until he had regained his senses.

"And you first realised something was wrong when this Mr Bartholomew started… 'shrieking'… I think, was the word used… to describe his reaction when he found the body?"

"Yes, sir."

"I'm sorry, but could you once again describe to me the events that led up to the discovery. I know you've given them to us before, but I would appreciate it if you could repeat it all again."

"Yes, sir. Of course, sir." Drawing a breath, Ali continued. "Every year, before dinner is served for this ball, I always do a pre-dinner staff briefing in the kitchen which takes at least thirty minutes. The fireplace is lit about forty minutes or so before the guests enter the dining room, so that the whole room is warmed up by the time the guests enter. It's usually lit by a junior waiter who is not fully involved with the dinner service."

Deducing that the S.P. may not know a thing about the science of lighting a fire, him being from the plains, Ali launched confidently into the details.

"We trained this new waiter on the setting up of the fires in the club. You see, we only have one youngster who was trained for this task, so we wanted a second in case the current chap left or was on leave. It was this dead boy, Siva, who was trained to be 'number two fire boy'. It took us quite a few months to train him properly because we have so many fireplaces here, of very different sizes. The dining room fireplace is very large in comparison to the ones in the common areas and the rooms."

Well into his pet subject of fireplaces now, Ali picked up some of his old confidence as he continued to hold forth. "Sadly, sir, few people realise that a successful fire starts with the correct construction of the hearth and the chimney, and another thing people don't realise is that not just anyone can build a fireplace. There's a proper science to it. The hearth and chimney must have the correct proportions. If not, you'll never get a fire to pull up into the chimney, no matter what you do or how experienced you are... am I boring you, sir?"

"No, no, not at all, carry on."

In actual fact, Ali had no idea that the S.P. was enjoying himself. For the first time since the night of the murder, Sundar was absorbing the atmosphere of the club, as snippets from his grandfather sprang up. With a twinge, Sundar pictured his grandfather sitting in the Ooty Country Club dining room, fifty years ago. He must have sat in front of that very fireplace during all those lunches and dinners he enjoyed there. He would never have imagined that his grandson would one day be investigating a brutal murder in that very room.

"So, as I was saying, sir, in the first place, it has to be built correctly. I remember being told as a young man that the building contractors from the plains neither had the skill nor the appreciation of the nuances involved, even when the proportions were…" Ali trailed off. He suddenly realised, with horror, that the belittling of building contractors from the plains would be considered a slight.

However, before his anxiety took hold, the S.P. spoke. "And, you were saying?"

"Quite. Yes, sir, as I was saying, once you have a correctly built fireplace, you can start learning about how to lay the wood correctly and then there's the kerosene and newspaper bits they have to understand. The fire must breathe, or else it will never take. This means that the correct laying of the wood must be taught to these boys. They must get the hang of how much and how to lay for each hearth size. It takes time. Siva had only just started on his own without needing supervision and now see what's happened." Ali winced at his last words, but there was nothing he could do to take them back now.

"I see, so you instructed Siva to light the fire?"

"Yes, at about seven-thirty I told him to start the fire. I wanted it blazing by eight-forty or so. We hoped to serve dinner between eight forty-five and nine p.m., although Mrs. Ponnappa was wanting it on at about eight-thirty. It's difficult for us to actually commit to an exact time as our staff are not trained for these large gatherings."

"And how long did it take him to start it up?"

"About twenty minutes or maybe a bit more. I can't say exactly as I was in the kitchen."

"So, I can put Siva down in the dining room from approximately seven-thirty to eight p.m.? Correct?"

"Definitely, yes. Sir, the thing with these junior chaps is that they dawdle a lot... seven-thirty to them can easily become seven forty-five. But I can confidently say that he was inside until about eight as I was in the room, finishing my inspection, when he left."

"From the notes we have, it seemed you asked him to go back inside a short time later?"

"Yes, sir. You see, after the fire was fully underway, I received a message from Mrs. Ponnappa requesting us to not light a fire. She said it was an unusually warm evening, so I sent him in again at about eight-twenty to stop the fire. To be precise, sir, I received Mrs. Ponnappa's message a few minutes after Siva returned to the kitchen. I was about to start my briefing and that got delayed because of the message, but when we looked for him, he couldn't be found. We thought he had gone to the bathroom. He turned up at about eight-twelve to eight-fifteen, and by the time he was sent back in again with full instructions, it must have been close to eight-twenty."

Shifting in his chair, Ali wondered if he should offer the S.P. more than just the coffee that had duly appeared, but then again, maybe not. It could look like a bribe. His wandering thoughts were interrupted by the S.P. clearing his throat.

Concentrating, Ali continued, "It's not an easy job. One has to pour water over the fire, which is a messy job, especially when it had taken so well. It would have taken him a full ten minutes or so to put it out and clean up any wet ash dripping off the hearth. Yes, a very messy business, sir."

"Right, so, in our notes, Mr Rasheed, it says no one was allowed into the dining room. For what period of time was that? We need an exact timeline, you see."

"Absolutely. Yes, of course. Before I do the briefing in the kitchen, I do an inspection in the dining room and then we bolt the dining room doors so that guests don't come in before all the food is placed. Otherwise, they wander in and start picking at the canapés which are usually all laid out by the caterers earlier on."

"I see, and at what time did you bolt the doors that night?"

"Yes, sorry, I finished my inspection at about eight-oh-five or so. I can't be sure exactly, but I bolted the doors at the same time because I wanted to start with the kitchen briefing immediately."

"So, that would be from eight-oh-seven, let's say to…?"

"Well, under normal circumstances, it would have been from eight-oh-seven, as you say, to when dinner was served, anytime between eight forty-five and nine p.m., sir."

"And this time, the doors were only opened after the body was discovered?"

"Yes, sir," sighed Ali.

"Could you give me the details running up to the discovery?"

Pulling his jacket lapels together, Ali wished he was anywhere but here, in front of this chap. He couldn't fathom the man at all. He seemed interested in what he was saying but at the same time seemed far away. Was it a ruse? Was it one of their 'interview tactics' to make him relax and rattle away? Shaking himself out of his mild panic, Ali realised it would be just a few minutes more before the S.P. was done. A comforting wave swept over him as he decided that, after the interview, he would go back to his room, have a hot shower, and a nice hot meal.

"Mr Rasheed…?"

"Sorry, sir. I was trying to get the events straight in my head before I spoke."

"I understand, Mr Rasheed." Sundar smiled at him.

Ali's eyes widened slightly. He now knew he was absolutely right; this was another one of their ploys. They don't mean it when they smile at you. They're just trying to get you to let down your guard.

Rallying himself, Ali continued, "I was at the end of the briefing when I heard a terrible noise from the dining room. It was a wail and, at the same time, a scream. I was shocked. A few of us rushed in. Bartholomew was sitting on the floor next to the…" He tapered off as the S.P. held up a hand to stop him.

151

"Before we go further, what was Bartholomew doing inside the dining room and what time did he go in?"

"Ah, yes. Sorry, sir. I forgot to mention that. I was coming to the end of the briefing. It was already just past eight forty-five and it looked like dinner would only get on just after nine, way past Mrs. Ponnappa's wishes. With respect, sir, it's very difficult dealing with these ladies if you can't manage the timeline they give you.

"They get very het up and don't stop talking about it for weeks together. I just wanted to give it all a final push. I realised that Siva hadn't returned from putting out the fire, so I told Bartholomew to go in, check that Siva had done a neat job, and yank the boy out. I also thought that Siva may have finished and was wasting time ogling the canapés. Poor boy must have already died. Bartholomew, in his younger days you know, used to be 'number one fire boy'. So, as I was saying, all our food was ready and piping hot; I never brief the kitchen staff who work directly on the stoves as it delays things. Only the service staff, you see, and laying out the food would take just a few minutes. Then the doors could be opened. So, to answer your question, Bartholomew went in at about eight-fifty and a few moments later we heard the commotion."

"I see. That period is now clear to me. How did these Ponnappas get to be the first guests on the scene?"

"I'm not really sure, sir. What I think happened is that Mrs. Ponnappa must have sent her son in to ask me when dinner was being served, maybe? The use of mobile phones isn't allowed inside the clubhouse, you see, and I think because the dining room doors were bolted, Mr Leo would have had to come in through the kitchen door that leads in from outside the building. Meaning he would have had to go outside, around the building, and in through the kitchen door, then through the kitchen to the dining room where he would have found us. All the kitchen staff by that time had come into the dining room, you see."

"I get the full picture now. We've taken all the details of who exactly the club employees are and who was on duty that night. Thank you for your time, Mr Rasheed. We'll be in and out, of course, until this is solved."

Ali nodded mutely.

Chapter Twenty-Three

Interview Aftermath

The Ootacamund Country Club

No sooner had Ali returned to his room were his dreams of a steaming shower and a relaxed evening dashed by a phone call.

It was Brigadier Johnny Chacko. "Ali, everything okay?"

"Yes, sir, thank you." Ali sat down, wondering what this call was going to entail.

"Good, good. Now the thing is, we should think of opening the club up for 'business as usual' by Saturday, at the latest, in my opinion."

Before Ali could respond, the Brigadier continued. "Saturday will make it a week since this death, and we need to start the ball rolling again. We can't hide our heads in the sand any longer."

"I agree, sir, but the staff are still very shaken up. I'm not sure how many will return to work by Saturday."

"Well, you'll have to go through the list and see about shoring up the weak ones, Ali. I know it won't be easy, but you know we have a full house in the next ten days or so, and one of them is General Vartak."

There was silence from Ali. In his heart, he knew that no matter what he said or promised or assured the staff, the fact was, they were downright terrified. Why shouldn't they be? After all, there was a vicious killer in their midst.

Surprisingly sensitive to Ali's silence, the Brigadier picked up the conversation once again.

"The thing is, Ali, this terrible incident won't be erased from their minds for a very long time. Certainly not until the murderer is caught, and that may never happen. Let's be realistic. If the killer is never caught, the best that we can hope for is that they get their confidence back in time, given, of course, there are no more murders. I very much doubt there will be. It's as clear as daylight that someone had a grudge against this poor boy and did the deed. So, I realise that the only thing that will give them a sense of security is to have some guards on the premises. I have a good friend, an ex-army major, who has a security company in Coimbatore. Most of his employees are ex-army, very well-trained chaps, very fit men. They'll be in plain clothes, unobtrusive, and with a brief from the committee and yourself on what's required from them. I guarantee the staff will feel secure."

Ali felt a dead weight had been lifted as he heard the Brigadier's words. Ali's trusted club president, Brigadier Chacko, had got to the heart of the problem along with a solution. Now, for the first time since Siva's murder, Ali was quickly beginning to feel his old self again.

Life may finally be returning to normal.

Buxey Lodge

The mist was thick, white, and moving in quickly from the valley below, almost like a creature on a mission. Sherry knew that in a matter of minutes her garden would disappear from sight.

Oh well, this is why we love these good old mountains so much, she thought. Life is a constant move from one season to the other. And as if five distinct seasons weren't enough, there was still another, albeit murky, short sharp monsoon in November to contend with. Sherry sighed, once we're over that one then our glorious winter will start. She smiled at the thought of Christmas.

Now, back to the big worry on hand. What state was Ali in? Should I go and visit him? An old friend like him can't be left in the lurch at this time. After all, he didn't have many friends, thanks to his reserved nature.

Yes, a reserved nature, just like her father. John Darling's personality was very similar to Ali's. Even his job was similar, as he ran four guest houses for the Germans working on the project in the seventies. Most of Sherry's successes in her career were thanks to her father. She diligently implemented into her daily routine his favourite mottos for 'achieving something in life, my girl', as he used to say. His definite favourite was 'God helps those who help themselves'. She realised that now she was no longer in the workforce, she had let go of these principles; forging a path forward was no longer a requirement to thrive. Perhaps she ought to reinstate these values. Biting the bullet, she decided to go over to the club and sit with Ali for a chat, whether he liked it or not.

Willowbund Police Station

Sundar was back at his desk and sorting out his notes from his interview with the club secretary. He had gone to the club alone as Iqbal was busy questioning Siva's friends in town.

He was convinced that this bludgeoning was a spur-of-the-moment decision by the killer. From what he had been told by Ali Rasheed, the timing of Siva's presence in the dining room was entirely based on instructions given to him, which meant that only Ali Rasheed would know exactly when the boy was inside, on both occasions. And what did that mean? Did he, or an accomplice, go in and kill the boy? Could the secretary have slipped away for a moment? The kitchen staff may not have noticed, especially if he slipped away for a moment before the briefing started, given the pre-banquet chaos in the kitchen. Between the two sessions in the dining room, Siva was missing for a good ten minutes. Had he seen something that caused his death just minutes later?

There was definitely something hanging in the air when he was with the secretary. He couldn't put his finger on it. Could just be nerves but he wasn't going to write it off just yet.

Shivering, he got up to put on a jacket. He once again felt disconcerted. This murder is unlikely to be about Siva, unless he did see, or know, something worth killing for. All the reports had him down as a bright youngster, quick to pick up as he went along. He may just have been too sharp for his own good.

And what a strange setting the crime was committed in, a club full of people, an enormous party going on. And a poor youngster murdered in the midst of it all. This meant, to the intuitive Sundar, that the killer was most probably a maniac.

Chapter Twenty-Four

Possession Lane

"Do you remember how Aunty Hannah always used to say that Catholic priests are the best for exorcism?" asked Sherry.

"Yes, of course I remember! How can any of us forget? Constantly fascinated with all that sort of thing she was. She swore she could see spirits and Dad attested to that fact. He said she was exactly like granny, and we all know about her, don't we? Anyway, I still think it's a creepy name for such a pretty pathway to be called 'Possession Lane'!"

"Honestly, Zee, I think it gives it character and a sense of history. After all, it's just a titchy lane. A strong name props it up. Anyway, do you remember the story?"

"Sort of. I remember the story very vaguely, tell me?" They were sitting in her bedroom and having had dinner, they were now winding down with a deliciously sweet Riesling.

Sherry was finally getting into the mood of the conversation; putting her feet up on the footstool, and shuffling herself into a comfy position, she said, "I guess I must have been about twelve years old... or thirteen, not sure but old enough to just about understand the gist of it all."

"Yes?"

"Well, they were all just talking one evening. It seems it was Father Machado who did the exorcism, and it was on a young girl. She was a Hindu. They said that her family were agriculturalists. She had a dad, a mum, and a younger brother." Sherry paused.

"And?"

"Hang on, I'm trying to remember... It's a bit sketchy. Oh yes, it's all coming back. There was another family, neighbours I think. There was a land dispute, neighbours were Catholic. Anyway, it wasn't a big issue. They weren't shoving each other or shouting but there was quite a bit of animosity over where the boundary lay. So, this was going on for a while. I'm guessing a few months, and then, this is the interesting part, one day the daughter came home from school and she, unbelievably, went down on all fours, crept under the dining table, and flatly refused to come out."

She continued, "Her parents were at home to witness this eerie behaviour, apparently her face was expressionless. They thought that she had probably been told off at school and was upset but when she refused to crawl out later that evening, they had to drag her out. By all accounts, she then started speaking in tongues and, scary this is, in a completely different voice! Almost like a man's voice. You can imagine how frightened the parents were. But, but, BUT, they were really smart. They knew exactly what they were looking at. The dad immediately went to The Hermitage and begged Father Machado to go home with him straightaway."

"He was such a kind man," sighed Zareen.

"Yes, lovely man. Of course, he went immediately with the girl's dad."

"And then what happened?"

"I don't know, to be honest. I suppose he must have put a cross on her forehead. And prayed? I think they get them to hold a Bible to their chest as well."

"You mean, it got sorted out then and there?"

"No, I think he had to go back to the house for two or three days consecutively, but yes, she was absolutely fine by the end of it."

"And the neighbours?"

"Left. Packed up and left that very week, which is why people think they had something to do with it."

"So where is this girl now, and the family?"

"The house is still there. There's an elderly couple living there, alone. Must be the parents, I'm guessing, but maybe not. After an incident like that, they may have wanted to move away. Then again, I might be wrong. But it's the same house and the same plot of land is being tilled, carrots followed by cabbages followed by potatoes and back to carrots again. No sign of the girl. She must have moved away, got married, and all that. Don't think the brother is there either."

With a sceptical look on her face, Zareen asked doubtfully, "How do you know so much about these people and about the couple still living there, even down to what they're growing, Sherry?"

"Because I always use that lane when I'm hopping around town and can't be bothered to use the car. Parking slots are a pain to find. Once I've got one, that's it.

Everything else is on foot. It's useful from the back of the market to that line of tailoring shops. What I do is park at the back of the market. The lane starts a little away from there; although it's just a few quick steps to get to the lane, it's another world once you're on it, with that valley dipping on the right with those luscious fields. You wouldn't for the life of you think you were minutes from the noisy market area. Once you take the side path from the lane, you're at the tailors in a blink. Walking the whole length of the lane will take about thirty minutes and, you know, it has those four or five side paths, all about five minutes from each other leading into town on the left side of it. They all lead into different areas in town, but you know all this, of course."

"Actually, I don't. I've never been on that path before."

They fell silent, sipping their wine and occupied with their own thoughts.

They could hear the start of the monsoon wind. Over the next few days, it would pick up momentum and howl away all night.

"What started us talking about the lane anyway, Zee?"

"You said you were on the path today as it's shorter to get to the club that way from Francis's place."

"Oh, yes. So, as I was saying, before we veered off onto the why and wherefore of its name, this afternoon I made up my mind to go see Ali. I just had to see him, to see how he was after that bloody awful mess."

"How was he? He must be terribly worried."

"Yes… so, as I was saying, I first went to drop off those DVDs we borrowed from Francis as it had brightened up quite a bit from the mist we had in the afternoon. Francis said that it'll probably be the only nice evening left before the monsoon takes hold. So, I decided to walk to the club. It only takes a few minutes from The Hermitage. Mary uses it all the time in good weather to get to the club; very proud she is of her constant to-ing and fro-ing four times a day."

"I know, she loves talking about it. She's so excited about getting onto the committee. I really hope it happens, so nice to have someone who we can relate to and who'll understand all our little complaints. I mean, I really can't be bothered to tell any of the men on the committee a single thing. It's all in one ear and out the other, with a vague look as if to say, 'I have bigger fish to fry, Zee'. Anyway, how is Ali and what did he say?"

"It was quite funny actually, but it's rude of me to laugh. I really did barge into his badly needed down-time, by the look of things."

"Oh?"

"Yes, he was drained and didn't look pleased to see me at all. Silly of me to think he would welcome me with open arms. Anyway, after a few minutes, he seemed to warm up to having some company. He's quite a lonely type of person, Zee, and quiet, too. They say it's the quiet ones that suffer the most."

Immune to Sherry's maudlin tone, Zareen asked, "So, did he discover the body? Was he the first on the scene?"

"No, it was Bartholomew! He went in and started screaming when he saw Siva. It was his screaming we could hear when Leo opened the dining room doors. Very unbecoming of a man to be screaming but I guess after the shock of having discovered AJ, it was enough to give him a nervous breakdown!"

"Just imagine Bartholomew's bad luck, Sherry, two deaths in a span of a month or so? Very oddly coincidental."

"Well, yes, exactly what I was thinking too, although strangely Ali didn't mention the coincidence of it. But first, put all that aside. This whole thing brings me back to what I've been saying… two deaths, one an outright murder, both in the club just weeks apart. They must be connected, in fact, Zee Zee, I insist that they're connected. You all have to back me up on this!" Sherry giggled.

"I'm beginning to agree, especially with the common denominator being Bartholomew. I can't help but feel there's something here, which as you say, we aren't able to put our finger on."

"Do you think Bartho was set up to discover the bodies? I mean, it couldn't have been him that killed Siva… at least, I don't think so. Not capable, is he, Zareen?"

"Who knows? None of us really know him but what reason would he have to kill Siva, unless that boy knew something? Mary's always saying there's all sorts going on at the club. There could be a scam going on. Maybe Bartho is involved in something?"

"I don't know what to think and more importantly, what the link between the two deaths could be, but guess what? When I went to see Ali, he had just finished a marathon interview with none other than the new S.P. that we've all been hearing about!"

"I wish he had interviewed us, Sherry. We only got his deputy asking us questions. Pity because he's gained quite a reputation. Anyway, how did the interview go?"

"Bloody awful, according to Ali. He said the S.P. looked like he was somewhere else altogether, so he's

164

worried about whether he had written down his account correctly or if he is going to botch it up and have Ali on the mat for something or the other."

"I doubt it very much. He's the one who caught Sunaina Rao's killer in Chennai. You couldn't have forgotten that story about that actress? Stabbed, I think she was."

"Yup, he's the one. He came out of that very well, and I think he's very smart too. I don't think those types get solutions simply out of thin air. You know, Zee Zee, I think I'll go pay him a visit. After all, I was in the dining room. The S.P. should have interviewed me just like he did the others. No doubt Johnny told them that I had just peeped in for a moment and so he thought I was inconsequential. Do you think that's what it was? I shall demand the right to be interviewed by him!"

"Okaaay, Sherry, whatever. I'm more interested in how people can get others possessed. Don't the evildoers just chant something into thin air and 'it all happens'?"

Chapter Twenty-Five

The S.P. and Bartholomew

Willowbund Police Station, eleven a.m.

"They should be here any minute, sir. Mr Rasheed called to say they left the club at least twenty minutes ago."

Sundar's deputy, Iqbal Khan, was quite sure that once this last interview was over, his boss would start the ball rolling. D.S.P. Khan held the new boss in great esteem. Sir was quite unlike the previous S.P., a bad-tempered man who, thankfully, was transferred barely eight months into the job. "Thanks, Iqbal, I hope we get this case closed soon. The chances of solving it will decrease as time goes by."

"I know, sir, the quicker we get on, the better." Khan left the S.P.'s office, keen to see whether the interviewee had, at last, arrived.

Willowbund Police Station, eleven-fifteen a.m.

Bartholomew stood apprehensively in front of the S.P.'s enormous desk. He was tallish, at least six feet tall, with slightly hunched shoulders. His face was long, thin, and gaunt. His eyes were slightly red, and he kept shuffling his

166

skinny legs. Standing confidently beside him was his friend, Daniel.

Sundar decided it was best he sat down, which, thankfully the man did without arguing, unlike most. Often as not, those being questioned by the S.P. seemed to feel that to remain standing was a show of deference, hence the onslaught of questions may well be shortened or softened.

Sundar gestured to the other chair for Daniel to sit in which, thankfully, he also did with no fuss.

Sundar took a long hard look at the men. This was going to take time, he realised. It mattered not. Best to get as much as we can and as soon as we can from them, although technically it was just Bartholomew being interviewed today. Daniel had been thoroughly questioned earlier. The club secretary had called earlier to say that, although Bartholomew had sufficiently recovered and could now be questioned, could he please be escorted to the station by his lifelong friend and fellow waiter, Daniel.

Sundar took stock of the men sitting nervously in their chairs, noticing how warmly dressed they were, hand-knitted pullovers, no doubt knitted by women in the family, thick scarves wound around their necks. Sundar realised those were exactly what he should invest in, pullovers and scarves. The thick jackets worn over his shirt weren't quite doing the job.

Before he could say anything, Daniel said in a hoarse whisper, "None of us did it, sir. We are all one family at the club. Mr Ali will tell you."

Bartholomew piped up, "Yes, sir. We all of us is a family and Mr Ali is just like our daddy. We won't any one of us hurt each other, sir."

Before Sundar could acknowledge this statement, Daniel spoke. "Anyone will tell you, sir, it wasn't us who killed Siva. It must be one of the caterers, sir. They were inside the dining room alone with Siva. We are not allowed in after the caterers start their work inside, no, not allowed."

Once again, the S.P. was stopped from speaking as Bartholomew said, "That lady came in to see the set-up. SHE might have done it."

Daniel continued, "Mr Aiden was in there alone after they left. Sir, he could have done it too."

There was a sudden silence. Sundar's thoughts were racing. What's this he was hearing? Two individuals, both caterers, had been seen inside the dining room alone with the victim? No one had mentioned this before. He saw Iqbal making a note of this.

Although Sundar hadn't a chance to get a word in edgewise, he decided that the outflow of information coming from these two may well be worth him keeping mum for some time.

"Siva was a good boy, sir. He did as we told him, and he did things properly. We are always telling Chinnaswamy to be careful and not spoil him. Chinnaswamy is always chasing girls, sir. We told him we don't want Siva getting into the same trouble like him."

Daniel interjected, "Yes, sir. We don't want any more trouble like all the firewood trouble that Ali, sir, had. He got very sick because of the things people were saying about him stealing firewood."

Sundar looked across at Iqbal with a raised eyebrow. However, yet again his train of thought was interrupted, as Daniel continued, "We was very busy, sir, and really tired even before the dinner serving started. We too tired to kill anyone."

"And I very, VERY tired, sir. After I saw Siva dead like that. After I saw Siva, sir, I thinking the Devil is chasing me. Yes, chasing me, sir."

"Because this is second time, sir, the caterers are there." Daniel deftly finished off Bartholomew's explanation of his extreme tiredness.

"So, it is ONLY caterers, sir, that done this."

The two interviewees sat back, taking a badly needed breath, greatly satisfied that they had been able to point the police in the right direction.

Sundar was now able to speak for the first time. "What do you mean by 'second time caterers are there'?"

"When Meester Panniker died, sir, the same caterers was there."

"Yes, and SHE was also there the whole evening."

"No, no, no, you're wrong Bartho-lo-miu. Yes, yes, SHE was there but those people also came in the nighttime, same time you find Meester Panniker dead, Bartho-lo-miu…"

"Iyooooo, De-ni-al, do you want to give me chest pain again?" wailed Bartholomew as he aggressively rubbed his chest.

Two p.m.

Sundar was perturbed. Someone named 'AJ Panniker' was found dead in his room some weeks before this murder. He had called Ali Rasheed to get more information on the circumstances but didn't get much. He got the feeling that this wasn't a subject the secretary wanted to delve into in any detail and he wondered why.

This was getting messy. Why were these waiters linking both the deaths? Because of the caterers? He had directed Iqbal to see them, a Pearl Veeraswamy and a Mr and Mrs. Screwallah. The Screwallahs will have to be questioned separately. He now did not know what to think but experience had taught Sundar to never disregard the seemingly simple opinion of the man on the street.

Chapter Twenty-Six

Glenealy House

Seven p.m.

"How nice to get together again! So good of you to organise this cosy evening, Bunny. I've been sooo looking forward to coming over."

Sitting down, Mary paused for a moment as she looked appreciatively around the beautiful room. An electric fire was blazing. Thank goodness, she thought, what with the wind outside howling like a banshee. This is just what's needed to comfort the soul.

"The Equestrian Ball turned out to be a bit of a damper for everyone, didn't it, Bunny? Thanks to that boy getting killed, a really shocking thing to have happened. Mind you, I don't mean to be rude about the club employees, but let's face it, it is what it is. When I get on the committee, I shall jolly well make sure there's proper discipline backstairs. This debacle can only be due to the shenanigans going on with the club staff."

Having had her say on the 'happening', as Mary would henceforth refer to the death of Siva Ranjan, she graciously accepted a glass of Laphroaig. She had arrived early and was eagerly awaiting the arrival of the other guests.

Downing her first refreshing sip, she asked Bunny who the guests were that evening.

"I'm afraid it's going to be a disappointing evening, Mary. Half of those I asked can't make it. Dimple rang this afternoon to say she's got a frightful headache, and Phyllis and Geoffrey can't come because an old friend has turned up who's only in town for this one evening. So, it's just us and the Buxey girls."

"Well, that's just lovely. It'll be far more intimate and interesting. I really haven't been able to get Sherry on the line for a proper chat about the 'happening', so I'm looking forward to a lovely 'feet up and chat evening'."

"But you missed the entire 'happening', Mary! Trust you to have pushed off before the murder."

"But not that much earlier, Bunny, from what I understand. The murder must have been committed just moments after I left. I'm not entirely sure, but that's what I'm hazarding from what I've heard. Such a pity. I could have been a great help. It seems it fell on poor Sherry to reorganise the dinner spread. I was able to have a couple of chats with her, but as I say, so much better to sit around with the whole evening ahead to talk about it."

The doorbell rang and within seconds, Bunny's glorious powder blue sitting room had the Buxey girls, as Bunny had named them, firmly ensconced alongside Mary. Drinks and home-made crisps were served.

Bunny looked around the room. She was positively glowing. These were her new friends and such dears they all were.

"It's my opinion we should try and figure out why on earth someone killed this fellow. There must have been a fight of some kind, for sure!" said Zareen.

"Well, if there was a scuffle, there would be remnants of it all around... broken china, for example. There wasn't any indication of a mess. Also, if there had been a fight, cleaned up or otherwise, there'd have been some evidence on the body, but the poor boy was just huddled on the floor with the poker next to him. Reminds me of that battered-to-death puppy I once found..." finished Sherry.

"Who could have done it? I certainly don't see a member of the staff creeping up on the boy and whacking him. That too, in the middle of all the hullabaloo of the dinner party about to kick off. No, no, no, it's not in their nature," replied Zareen, putting on her best authoritative medical voice.

"Really, Zareen, who knows what their nature would be when push comes to shove; we can't speak for them," huffed Mary.

A real closet snob, as I've always said, thought Sherry with an inward sigh.

"Surely you're not suggesting a club member or one of the guests did it?" asked Bunny.

At this point, Mary decided that enough was enough. "Dear girl, the boy was brand-new. No one knew him from Adam. Who on earth from the members' side would have wanted to kill an unknown chap? And don't forget, none of the guests were allowed anywhere near the dining room!"

Zareen now seemed to reluctantly agree that the staff could be involved. "It's a pity to decide on it being one of the staff but coming to think of it, we do have the club firewood boy holed up in our house saying he doesn't want to go back to work there because he's too scared. And he can't tell us why or who he's scared of or even what he's scared of, so, I guess... what does that mean I wonder?" Her voice was now meek and unsure, realising that she had very probably got the wrong end of the stick.

Sherry added, "And he usually stays at your home, doesn't he, Mary? But now he doesn't seem to want to go anywhere near there and we can only deduce it's because The Hermitage is so close to the club. Maybe he's scared someone will pop over from the club and whack him on his head, too."

"Has he said who he's scared of, Sherry? That might help in pointing the police in the right direction," Mary asked.

"We don't think he knows. Don't think he has a clue. You know what he's like. Very simple and ever so slightly 'off '. If, at some stage, he has a recall, it may only be fleeting. It will disappear again."

"If he's so scared, Sherry and Zareen, then it means he saw something, or knows something. Have you tried to ask him?" queried Mary.

"Actually no, we haven't, have you, Zee?" asked Sherry.

"Nope."

"I don't think there's any point really. He can be very vague, Mary. Surely you must have noticed, seeing as he's spent far more time at your house than he's ever spent at Buxey?"

"I agree. But you see, I have quite a different view altogether on it, and that's exactly because he spends time at home. I've seen him quite lucid at times, but as you've done, it may be best to let sleeping dogs lie. There's been enough of an upset all round as it is. And by all accounts, the new police chap is a smart cookie. He'll get around to figuring this out pretty soon, I'm betting."

"Yes, I think Mary's right, girls. Don't ask him too much. For all we know, he may well know, inadvertently of course, who the killer is. If that's let out of the bag, it's likely the killer will find out and that'll put him in danger and maybe you, too!" said Bunny.

"I think we can safely assume he doesn't know a thing anyway. He left the club that night as soon as his shift was over, so it's highly unlikely he knows anything," said Sherry.

"Too true, that, Sherry. Best to leave it all be, as Bunny says," advised Mary.

Nine p.m.

Bunny was now alone in her bedroom, her guests long gone. The Buxey girls left first, followed sometime later by Mary.

After seeing Sherry and Zareen off, Bunny and Mary sat in front of the fire nursing a cognac and chatting about the evening, about the club that Mary loved so dearly, about the 'happening', and about the poor firewood boy who was terrified, but sadly, didn't know what terrified him. It can only be a tortuous existence, they concluded.

Then Mary said something that not only reaffirmed Bunny's high regard for her, but also frightened her. Mary had said that she was sure the boy was resisting staying at Nun's Cross, not because he was scared of the club staff, but because he was scared of Francis Fonseca.

"It's just a feeling I have, dear... as I say, it's just a feeling."

Chapter Twenty-Seven

The Police and the Suspects

D.S.P. Iqbal Khan was extremely pleased that his notes, painstakingly compiled from the interviews, were now finally ready.

"All the paperwork on our suspects is here, sir," he proudly announced, pushing the file forward on the desk.

"Thanks, Iqbal. Just run me through them. It's much quicker."

"Of course, sir. The first is Bartholomew Solomon, he was first on the scene…"

He stopped midway as the S.P. interrupted him. "Let's get to him last."

"Yes, sir. Next on the list is Ali Rasheed. Second on the scene. The victim was sent in on his instructions. There is some confusion as some of the staff say that Rasheed disappeared from the kitchen immediately after Siva was sent to the dining room. When questioned, Mr Rasheed's reply is that he thinks he may have gone to the Gents but can't even remember if he did or not and, if he did, whether it was after Siva went in or quite some time before. He says he just doesn't remember."

"Well, it must have been chaotic in the kitchen. Do these people know for sure what they're saying, or did they simply lose him in the crowd?"

"Not sure, sir, could be. And then there are the caterers who were in and out at about that time too, adding to the numbers."

"But why would Rasheed kill the boy in the middle of all that chaos? And the answer to that, of course, brings us back to the same question, over and over again… that it could only be because of something that happened, or that shouldn't have happened, that the victim was privy to."

"Agreed, sir, but absolutely nothing is coming up that was untoward."

"It doesn't have to be untoward, Iqbal. At least, it wouldn't be untoward in the eyes of someone who saw, heard, whatever, simply because they had no clue. Any incident, seemingly normal to the ignorant, will be quite alarming to someone who knows better. Don't forget, even Rasheed, who didn't have much to do with the victim, says he was a very sharp youngster. Too smart for his own good probably. Anything else on Rasheed?"

"That's it, sir."

"So, we will conclude as of now: (a), no motive that we can ascertain; and (b) he had a small window in which he could have killed Siva, if what they say is correct in that he disappeared after sending Siva in. It depends on how desperate he was. Events might have forced his hand. Next."

"Caterers, sir, by the name of Screwallahs. Anna and Aiden. As Daniel Arthur and Bartholomew Solomon claimed, they really were inside when the victim was prepping the fire. In fact, they were in and out setting up their food during both times that the victim was sent in."

"Motive? None, I'm sure."

"Correct, sir, but there are comments from the kitchen staff to say Mr Screwallah went in again quite some time after they finished their job. Went in alone and was inside the room for about five minutes."

"Bartholomew found the body at about eight-fifty, which means this Aiden chap should have been inside killing him just before. Unless that exact time is established and, of course, a motive, we can't haul him up for more questioning. I don't think we will get an exact time from him for his second visit to the dining room; he won't tell us even if he does know. If he killed the boy, he will want to be vague. If he didn't kill the boy, he will still want to be vague in case we pin it on him. Where was the wife when he went in alone?"

"In the van, sir."

"What van?"

"Their company delivery van. The company's slogan is 'Scrumptiousness from the Screwallahs' with the 's', 'c', and 'r' in bold, sir."

D.S.P. Khan's amusement seemed to wash over the S.P. "Do you mean to say that this information about the wife in the van is also from the kitchen staff?"

"Yes, sir."

"They seem much sharper than expected. What did this Aiden person say about going in alone?"

"He said, sir, that when he and his wife had finished, he had found a full tray in the van which hadn't been given in,

179

so he took it in to lay out. He claims that the boy was going into the dining room as he left."

"Sounds bona fide to me. Now, for Screwallah, we will have to conclude almost the same as we did for Rasheed: (a), no motive that we can ascertain; and (b), he had a small window in which he could have killed Siva. But you'll have to question the wife on what she says about his time away from her before we can conclude anything for this character. Next, there was another caterer?"

"Yes, her name is Pearl Veeraswamy, owner of a well-known cafe in town. She's the lady who, again it's the kitchen staff who say so, went in for a short while. But when we questioned her, she refuted this claim. Told us to speak to the head chef. His name is Nava. We spoke to him and although he corroborated what she said, his story is slightly different to hers. He says that, and this is claimed by both sides, when she first arrived with her items, she came to the door and handed over multiple trays to the chef requesting him to lay out the food as she wasn't feeling well. Which is what happened. She waited in her vehicle during the interim period. Then it seems she came back and picked up the empty trays, and he thought that was the end of that. But she turned up again, a full twenty minutes later, asking if she could go in to see how her items were laid out. The chef was about to let her in but as she took her first step into the kitchen, her mobile rang, and seeing the caller's name, which the chef didn't see, she said she didn't have time and left."

"Mmm… odd thing to have happened. Why was she hanging about for twenty minutes after picking up her trays? Did she explain herself?"

"Yes, but not to our satisfaction. Her version was that it wasn't twenty minutes, but more like ten minutes. She says it took her that much time to stack up her trays as she had a back problem. Then she got into her car and was about to drive off when she thought she would like to see her... I think she said 'merangs', so she went to speak to the chef but then decided she was too tired after all and left. When we asked about the phone call, she brushed it off, claiming it was a wrong number."

"Trace that incoming number, Iqbal. I want it quickly. We can't conclude anything with this lady until we get that number. Who is next?"

"We're back to Bartholomew again, sir. Nothing could be obtained from the staff about him having any connections with the victim, other than work related. No possible motive. By all accounts, he is fairly stable."

At this point he stopped and looked at the S.P. with amusement, who returned his look with a raised eyebrow and a grin.

Some semblance of humour has returned to the boss, thought Iqbal before continuing.

"There's no family to speak of. No wife, never married, no children."

"Doesn't look like he's the fellow though, sir. Seems very highly strung, extremely weak, and hysterical. After that heart rubbing performance, it was impossible to get any information from either of them, as you know, sir."

"Yes, it was, but I want to speak to someone who knows something about this AJ Panniker. Both those chaps claim there is some connection, although the doctor who was called in is emphatic it was natural causes. No autopsy was done, so we can't fully go by what he says. These chaps seem to think the two deaths are linked by a common factor, the caterers. Bartholomew found him dead, and it had a profound effect on him, so as I said, we must find someone to speak to regarding this first dead man."

"Yes, sir. Do you have anyone in mind?"

"No."

Chapter Twenty-Eight

From Buxey Lodge to Willowbund Police Station

Buxey Lodge, ten a.m.

"I must make an impact today. It's ridiculous how I've been side-lined and not properly interviewed, after all I was the one who saved the ball by pulling myself up and out of the mire and panic they remained firmly stuck in! Well, how do I look?" asked Sherry, with a twirl.

Zareen decided with a sigh that she ought to be blunt. "The lipstick has to be toned down. Didn't you know that bright red can frighten men?"

Giving Sherry the requisite 'once over', she was dismayed to note that she had bright red shoes on as well.

"No, absolutely not. I don't want to be shunted to the back of his mind along with all the others that were interviewed."

"If you say so. Be careful what you say, Sherry. Best not to allude to all sorts, what with this AJ thing going around and around in your head. Mind you, I'm coming around to that as well, but as I said, best to be circumspect. Especially as it's the police.

"And for goodness sake, don't give the impression that you're being petulant. It will put them off, or worse get their backs up."

"I know all that!"

Willowbund Police Station, ten-forty a.m.

"Who?"

"Miss Sherry Darling. She was one of the guests at the ball. She says she thinks we overlooked interviewing her."

"Overlooked? Was she? I remember the name somewhere in the notes."

"Not overlooked, sir. Don't know why she is claiming so and, you're right, we do have a statement from her."

"Doesn't matter. Tell her to come in as soon as she arrives."

Sundar couldn't for the life of him decide where or when he had heard the name Darling before. It rang a bell, albeit a very far away bell.

Willowbund Police Station, eleven forty-five a.m.

Sherry realised she had never been in a police station in her life. She was made to sit at the front desk area on a wooden bench. The room was busy and fairly noisy. There was a woman crying at the desk, whimpering quietly about her drunken son-in-law beating her daughter. On the other side of the room, a policeman was talking loudly on a walkie talkie, on a very crackly line, head half out of the window, hoping to reduce the noise level in the room. The opened window allowed a freezing cold breeze into the hall. The whole situation was very unsatisfactory but just as she started to list out the improvements needed, a dirty looking man wandered in then wandered out again. He was definitely homeless, by the look of his slightly matted hair and a face that hadn't had a shave for weeks. Shifting gingerly on the bench, she grimaced at the thought of the last occupant. She couldn't imagine working in a place like this. Unpleasant. And cold drafts coming in from every crack and gap… and wide-open windows. She wondered if there were jail cells in this building, as temporary holding points for culprits before they were sent off to proper jails. Her thoughts were cut off midway. A policeman appeared in front of her and, moments later, she was sitting in front of S.P. Raman.

Sherry was at a loss for words. She had been interviewed, after all. What really was her excuse to be insisting she should be interviewed again. Her ego? Yes, that was it, she realised glumly. The S.P. looked smart and alert, confirming all that she had heard of him. How was she to address him, she suddenly wondered with alarm?

"It seems you have something to say about the murder at the country club, Ms Darling?"

Sherry was grateful for the opening.

"Mmm… yes, mmm… sir… I was wondering if I should speak to 'someone' because I was actually inside the dining room when Siva was killed, meaning not when he was killed but after when his body was found. Along with the others, Brigadier Chacko, etc."

Sherry's non-existent confidence, from a few minutes ago, was now picking up very quickly. Her voice was now more sure of itself.

"I had heard that they were all interviewed by you personally, whereas I wasn't."

Sherry stopped. Doubt once again crept up. Her words sounded childish, even petulant, to use Zareen's words, and now her warnings flooded back too. What was she thinking, when the general intelligentsia avoided the police at all costs, she was pushing herself onto them? These people who could be brutal, unfair, cold. They could make your life difficult, very difficult. She should have taken a leaf out of Ali's book, been wary and cautious.

"You were interviewed by my deputy, D.S. Khan."

"Yes, yes, I was. I'm just wondering, you see, if I was given the same set of questions as the others at the crime scene? I think I may have been categorised as an observer rather than a prime witness."

Sundar raised an eyebrow. He knew the basic set of questions were the same for all, but she, of course, wouldn't know that, he concluded, with some charity. He also knew if she had something specific to say, she would have said it by now. She seemed to have an eagerness about her and as he had some time today, maybe having a chat with this lady might finally give him a glimpse as to the lie of the land up at the club, something that had hitherto been far from his grasp.

Sherry knew she was being sized up and, in turn, she wondered about the man in front of her. He must be a good decade younger than her. On the slimmer side more than muscular, his face had a frank look about it and she noticed his uniform was perfectly crisp, clean, and creased in all the right places... a certified 'c.c.c.'. Smiling to herself, she decided she would tell Zee his uniform was 'c.c.c.', or should it be 'c.c.c.c.', adding the 'certified'? She won't have a clue as to what I'm saying and will get irritated. She wondered if he was married or if he did his own laundry, or did officers of his rank have their uniforms delivered 'ready to wear' every morning?

"Why don't you give me a description of what you saw in the dining room?"

Startled, Sherry abandoned her thoughts on crisp uniforms and came back to the subject on hand. Cutting to the chase, she gave a quick description of the events leading up to her opening the kitchen door leading into the dining room and getting to the heart of the scene inside.

"... and I thought it was Chinnaswamy who had died. You wouldn't know him, but I was so sure it was Chinnaswamy and we even went home that night thinking it was Chinnaswamy."

It took another ten minutes of chatting before the S.P. got to the bottom of who Chinnaswamy was. The name wasn't on the list of those questioned because he wasn't on duty that night.

"So, he's now at our home, very frightened. Siva was his assistant, so to speak. He was training him on the side for the fire set-ups. He doesn't want to return to work now and doesn't want to leave our home either, not that we have a problem with him staying with us."

"In what context do you mean he's staying in your home?" Sundar thought it highly unlikely this woman would house a club firewood stacker in a guest bedroom

187

next to hers, indefinitely. Not that she seemed the snooty type... but, yes, highly unlikely.

"He's our maid's nephew, so he's staying in her quarters. We think it's odd he's not staying with his other aunt, where he usually goes for a few days. He keeps saying he's scared to go there but doesn't know why. He's mentally challenged, born like that. His mother, Clara, died in the double cyclone we had that November."

She realised, unlike the locals, he may not know which 'November' she was talking about, having just arrived here. The 2009 November disaster was loosely referred to by all as 'that November'.

Ignoring the November cyclone subject, Sundar asked, "So would you say your Chinnaswamy was a good friend of the victim?"

"Oh yes, and Siva adored him, latched onto his every word. Chinnaswamy positively basked in his adoration. Poor boy, it's unlikely he'll ever get anyone again to look up to him."

"We must see Chinnaswamy, but as he seems to be going through some kind of an episode, we'll send someone to your home to see him. In fact, I may see him myself."

"Gosh, yes, of course. This is my number," said Sherry eagerly, taking out a notepad to write it on, only to be told they had her number on file.

Chapter Twenty-Nine

The Bloomin' Bloom

Why Jasmine?

Arriving home, Francis covered his nose with his thick scarf and quickly ran up the few steps leading to his front door. Entering, he closed the door firmly.

Removing his scarf, he peeped into his sitting room to double check that all the curtains were firmly drawn, which they were. He knew the windows had been bolted closed hours ago. Nevertheless, he suspiciously sniffed the air and frowned. As expected, and despite all his efforts, he simply could not get rid of the heavy fragrance of jasmine. The jasmine vines outside, all four of them, were in full bloom and thriving in a very fertile bed right next to his front door, much to his disappointment.

He absolutely and utterly detested the strong scent of jasmine. Its sickly-sweet smell made him horribly nauseous, and the scent seemed to hang heavily in the air, thanks to the dampness and the constant monsoon drizzle.

Mary had been saying with great glee the other day that she had found a new 'double jasmine' variety and was going to be planting soon. He simply couldn't face an extra onslaught of this scent.

Ah, well, it's a good excuse to go out of town for a few weeks next year. I'll be able to skip some of this God-awful weather and this blasted bloom, he thought.

He remembered researching, at this time last year, why these jasmines were so auspicious for the Hindus. His maternal grandmother was a Hindu, but she hardly wore jasmine in her hair, thankfully. He couldn't find anything to explain the significance of jasmine in Hinduism, other than the fact that the white flowers signified 'purity', because of course they were white. Ridiculous, all this business of whiteness and lightness.

Francis went to his bedroom and sat in his armchair. He felt drained... the killing at the clubhouse, the chaos that ensued, the exhaustive questioning. His thoughts wandered to Siva, who had spent so much time at The Hermitage, hanging around with Chinnaswamy... running to open the gate for him every time his car drew up.

Why Not Jasmine?

The curtains inside Nun's Cross were only just being drawn.

Mary was sitting with an iPad, playing Sudoku, as Liza was getting the house ready for the evening.

There was a sniffle; Mary stopped playing.

"Liza, there's no point. I know it's difficult, but you must leave Chinnaswamy alone for some time. He is undergoing a lot of stress. He'll get better soon, I promise, it's just the shock. You have to be thankful that at least he wasn't at the club when it happened! Imagine how much more of a shock he would have been in if he had actually been there that night!"

Mary was exasperated; this was becoming a daily conversation with Liza.

"Yes, Ma, I understand but..."

"No 'buts', Liza. Just leave things. Why don't you go and visit him? Take tomorrow afternoon off. Philomena loves jasmine; take a whole basket of flowers to her and make Chinnaswamy's favourite ginger biscuits. You and Philo can string the flowers together while you all chat. It will be like old times. I'm sure getting back to normalcy will help him get better faster."

"Thanks, Ma! Are you sure about the flowers?"

"Yes, of course. Everyone loves jasmine!"

Chapter Thirty

The Monsoon

Ali Rasheed

Ali frowned as he trudged along. The ground was sodden, the grass was slippery, and he was cold.

Have to be careful... can't afford a fall on top of everything else I have to cope with, he thought anxiously as he hurriedly wiped the rain from his eyes and lashes. It didn't help that he had a wide brimmed hat on. The wind still managed to lash the rain across his face. He knew well enough that with such high wind, it was impossible to use an umbrella. It would just flip inside out.

He was returning to the clubhouse from the firewood shed, having gone to check that it was fully stocked and that there were no roof leaks. This non-stop rain permeated everything... and damp firewood was his worst nightmare.

He consoled himself that in another few minutes he would be indoors, dry and warm. The thought of a roaring fire lifted him.

The weather was treacherous. The rain had not abated. The days had become miserably dark, and the wind was at gale force level, picking up even more momentum at night.

The southwest monsoon had well and truly set in, which meant that fires had to be lit. Thankfully for the club staff, the monsoon season was the time when they hardly had any guests staying in, but local members had started frequenting the club after it had opened its doors. That meant that the fireplaces in the lounge, the bars, and the dining room had to be lit. Brigadier Chacko had helped to arrange, through his army connections, two temporary men, supposedly with some experience in this 'field' but, as he had expected, they weren't up to the mark by a long shot and had to be supervised by none other than Bartho.

Sundar Raman

Sundar Raman and Iqbal Kahn got out of the police jeep and dashed into the station. They had just returned from the western countryside and were frozen stiff. It had also been a wasted trip.

"We can't do anything about this complaint until the weather clears up completely, Iqbal," said Sundar as he made his way to his office.

He sat down, hoping that a hot cup of coffee would appear. He was recovering both from extreme cold and the breathtaking scenery he had experienced that morning.

They had set out early to deal with a slew of complaints from the Todas, the tribe that owned thousands of buffaloes that were allowed to freely graze on hundreds of acres of wilderness. Sadly someone, or some people, were randomly killing their buffaloes.

He closed his eyes for a moment, determined to once again visualise the never-ending grasslands that formed gentle mounds which dipped into shallow valleys, that in turn were filled with trees and streams.

He had never seen such a heavenly setting in his life. It seemed unreal; the vegetation was mainly shola trees which only grew in the numerous little valleys. On the grass mounds, short bushes were scattered about at random.

The land was geographically completely different from that which surrounded Ooty town, and again, completely different from the mountainous approach through the Ghat road on the other end of the range. Unfortunately for them, though, they had barely reached their first stop when they had to turn back due to thick fog. Knowing there was no point in battling on and probably setting themselves back many hours, they returned.

His coffee arrived, and a few minutes later Iqbal came in to say that he had his report ready, tying up the loose ends on what the caterers had claimed when they were questioned.

"And what, exactly, are they saying?"

"Sir, we spoke to Anna Screwallah who, at first, couldn't even recall her husband's absence after they had finished up at the clubhouse, but then, after much thinking, finally did. She said that as soon as she got into the van, she was 'on her phone'. Remembers the husband shutting the van doors at the back. Then it seems he came to her side of the van to say 'he'll be back in a minute', but now, as she thinks about it, she thinks he was actually away anywhere between twenty to thirty minutes. In fact, sir, we had to question the husband first because the 'wrong' number phone call that Ms Veeraswamy claims she received was not a wrong number. It was a proper phone call from Aiden Screwallah."

He paused for effect but then carried on when he got no reaction from his boss.

"When we spoke to Mr Screwallah, he begged us not to tell his wife, and said he was just having a 'little thing' with Ms Veeraswamy. And when we spoke to her, she confessed, but said it was only 'a casual fling'. We did tell her that it was being put on record that she had deliberately lied to the police. She got quite upset when she heard this and said that as Mrs. Screwallah is a friend of hers, she was compelled to lie because she didn't want her to hear about it."

"So, I suppose Screwallah sticks to his story that he was inside the dining room for roughly five minutes and the rest of the time was with Pearl Veeraswamy behind a bush somewhere?"

"Yes, sir. That's the story of the screwing caterers." Iqbal's attempt at humour, once again, fell on deaf ears.

"Hmmm… you know what that means, don't you?"

"No, sir."

"Mrs. Screwallah doesn't have an alibi either."

"Oh, yes. You're right, sir. I didn't think of that."

Chapter Thirty-One

From Willowbund to Buxey

"And is that the house, sir?" asked Iqbal as he leaned out of the car window.

"I think it must be," replied Sundar as his eye caught an enormous jacaranda on the side of the drive leading to Buxey.

Sherry had left a definite impression on Sundar the day she had barged into his office, insisting on giving her version of the events on the night of the murder. She struck him as the 'what you see is what you get' type of girl. After she left, he couldn't, for the life of him, get her surname out of his head. He knew that he had heard the name somewhere, but where, he knew not. The next day he had an inkling that maybe his grandfather had mentioned it, so he called his mother to check. She confirmed that, yes, he spoke of a John Darling many times, mostly along with another name, Farzan Mistry, owner of a large house named Buxey Lodge. It turned out that Farzan Mistry's brother was married to John Darling's sister-in-law and that Sundar's grandfather had visited Buxey Lodge a number of times.

Sundar narrated the story to Iqbal as they drove to Buxey and instructed him not to let on to the ladies as he didn't want any distractions until the investigation was over.

In his heart though, Sundar was pleased. Even though the ladies were clueless of this fact, he felt that the connection with the past was a strong and positive sign. The unlikely character that was Sherry Darling could well turn out to be the ally he now needed.

He was acutely aware that there was not much they were likely to get from Chinnaswamy, given his mental state, but one never knew. After all, the most innocuously uttered word could solve a case.

His main aim today was to get as much as possible on AJ Panniker from the very chatty Ms Darling. Two deaths, in the span of just weeks, must mean they were connected. He knew that if he found out exactly what had happened to this AJ Panniker, then they may well solve Siva's murder.

The men were welcomed at the front door by an enthusiastic Sherry and Zareen.

They settled down in the sitting room and were served tea and shortbread.

Having dispensed with the initial niceties, Sundar felt he could now plunge into the pressing matter on his mind.

"I'm interested in knowing more about the person who died at the club some weeks ago. We heard about him from the club waiters, Bartholomew and Daniel. An 'AJ Panniker'? Did you know him?"

Whatever he expected in response, it was certainly not the highly voluble reaction he received.

Sherry and Zareen started talking at once, oblivious to the two bemused men.

"… and I kept telling her not to be silly, 'you're just imagining things'. But after this poor boy got killed and especially as our Bartho found both bodies, I can't help but agree with Sherry… it's almost as if someone set it up so that he would find both bodies, in the hope this would push Bartho off the edge!"

"Zee, there are many easier ways to push Bartho over the edge than to kill two people, surely! I think it's just coincidence that he found them both, but I don't think he had anything to do with their deaths," finished Sherry, emphatically.

Sundar felt a sense of déjà vu… this was fast going the same way as his interview with the waiters. Never mind, unlike the earlier one, this wasn't a formal session.

After a few minutes, he was finally able to get in a word. "So, you've both been under the impression that the AJP death was not natural?"

"Oh yes, Sherry always, always, thought there was something suspicious about AJ's death. He was such a creep, a very unlikeable man, brash and arrogant, too."

Sherry cut in, "Yes, and he had hardly been in town for two days when he died, so doesn't that show that he must have upset someone… and that 'someone' did him in?" She finished in a conspiratorial whisper, almost as if the 'someone' might have been in the next room.

"How though, Sherry?" asked Zareen excitedly, eyes glinting.

The general volume in the room was increasing along with a sense of high drama.

Sundar decided to interject before Sherry could theorise. "Is it possible for you to recount what transpired in the two days he was in town?"

"Well, from what we heard, he came straight up to the country club and checked himself in. The next day, or the day after, not very clear on this point, was the annual summer garden party at the club, which is called 'The President's Tea'. We weren't there but we've heard from first-hand sources that he really threw his weight around. Hobnobbing with only the crème de la crème, turning his nose down at the plebians, and so on. But worst of all was his declaration to everyone, plebians included, that he was redeveloping the Chater Hall property and going to call it Chater Mall of all things! All the Fonsecas were right there when he said this, can you just imagine?"

Of course, the men couldn't 'imagine' it, having no knowledge of either the Fonsecas or Chater Hall. Although the name Fonseca definitely rang a bell.

"Weren't there a few Fonsecas at the club on the night of the murder?" asked Sundar, turning towards Iqbal.

"Two, sir."

Sherry corrected the Fonseca head count by explaining that the Violet Reddy on their list was also a Fonseca, before her marriage.

Zareen added, "Yes, absolutely. All three siblings were there. The Fonsecas are an old Ooty family, and they were the original owners of Chater Hall."

After spending a few minutes acquiring the background on Chater Hall and AJP's connection to the property, they sat in silence, deep in thought.

Sherry broke the silence, "And this man was found dead in his room on the same night of the President's Tea party...

"What about Chinnaswamy? Do you want to see him in the kitchen or up here?" asked Sherry.

"Yes, we'll see him now, then we'll leave. We've taken up a lot of your time." replied Sundar.

They saw him in the kitchen, but it turned out that fifteen minutes was all that was needed. Chinnaswamy, as expected, was nervy and barely spoke, and had nothing new to add to their knowledge on Siva.

Returning to the sitting room, Sherry, noticing disappointment in the air, said, "His other aunt came by the other day, and he cheered up quite a bit. I think if he starts getting out of the house, he'll soon regain confidence. The trouble is, we can't understand why he is nervous to go out anywhere. He wasn't even at the club when the murder happened. He left at least a good hour or more before. We can't imagine what condition he would be in if he had been there!"

"Or, God forbid, if he had found the body!" added Zareen as she opened the front door for them.

"Well, did you see how smart their uniforms were?" said Sherry as she nibbled at leftover shortbread.

"I noticed him! Why didn't you tell me he was so good looking?"

"Oh, is he?"

Chapter Thirty-Two

The Clouds, the Fog and the Rain

Clouds

Sitting up in bed, Chinnaswamy was thinking of the two policemen from last evening. He wasn't scared of them.

Aunty Philo had told him clearly that they knew he had not done anything bad, but they had so many questions about Siva, most of which he couldn't answer.

Chinnaswamy told them he didn't know much about him. He knew they wouldn't be interested in the fact that Siva was his best and dearest friend and the only person who totally believed him when he said something, anything, no matter how small it was. And now he is gone, just like Mum. He knew he would never find another friend like Siva as long as he lived. Everyone around him, even his aunts, whom he knew in his heart loved him deeply, always looked slightly doubtful no matter what he was saying.

But the best thing this morning was that he was happier than he had been in days. Even though the police had come and asked so many questions about Siva, questions that brought back all his sadness, he still felt that a heavy cloud had been lifted from his head this morning.

Slow that he was, Chinnaswamy had instincts that could rival that of a psychic. He knew that the visit of his

Aunt Liza with his favourite ginger biscuits had made a huge difference to him. The heavy gloom and despair he was carrying seemed to fall away. He had been invited to stay with her for as long as he wanted to, even if it was for one night. She said it would make her happy, and it would make him happy too. He planned to go for two or three nights; he couldn't stay too long because Aunty Philo would miss him now that he had been staying in Buxey for so many days. He might have to spend half the month with each aunty from now on to keep them happy.

Her visit had made him feel good, almost as if this 'bad time' was now over. He felt lighter, stronger, and he even felt like getting back to work. He didn't know if Rasheed sir would take him back… he must be very angry.

Fog

Francis decided to let it go. After all, she is elderly and her brain is probably getting fogged up. She had obviously clean forgot that he couldn't abide the blasted flowers. No, she wasn't asking him to do this favour to rile him to the point where he would contemplate moving out. He thought back to the numerous times she had mentioned how pleased she was that he had rented the cottage, saying 'We don't have to worry so much about security now that you're here, Francis. With just poor little Liza and me here, we were quite defenceless'.

This morning, she had asked if he could pick up the jasmine plants from the nursery. Her driver was on leave, and she was worried about driving in the heavy fog. She needed a cataract operation by next year, she had been told, so it was best not to attempt anything silly. However, she did magnanimously offer to jump into his car with him, in which case she would go into the nursery to pick up the plants, thus alleviating him from at least one of the two chores. But he gallantly said not to worry, he would get it all done on time. "The thing is, Francis, the nursery had to order the jasmines in and they're arriving at about three, and as they are getting hardly any customers coming in, because of the weather, they've decided to close for a full week. You know the forecast is for heavy showers in the next few days."

He hated the thought of going to the nursery. Oblivious to his plight, she continued, breathless, eager. Poor old thing, he thought.

"They asked me to come by four as they want to close up by four-thirty, you know how dark it gets now. Is that okay for you, Francis? I hate to bother you but there's no one else…"

"No problem, Mary. I'll be there on time."

She was very grateful, giving him her old smile, something he had not been graced with for some months now.

Rain

Chinnaswamy had his thick green jacket on. He didn't need an overnight bag as he had enough clothes at his Aunty Liza's, but he did have a little cloth bag with his toothbrush and toothpaste, and most important of all, the bottle of hair gel that Siva had given him for his birthday.

He pulled his jacket close to his neck. It was missing a few buttons. He kept forgetting to tell Aunty Philo to sew them on. He had to walk quickly now, the drizzle was getting heavier, and he couldn't see much. There were car headlights behind him, which helped him to see down the path. They will start talking about Christmas. They always do in June. Christmas, Christmas, Christmas. Mary M'am is always saying 'but, my boy, it takes months to get it perfect, we have to start in June to get it right!' Then she'll say, 'don't worry, my boy, Mr Francis will help us put the tree up'.

He shuddered. An overwhelming feeling of anxiety gripped him again. He tried to shake it off. Christmas was his mum's favourite time of the year. He wished he could sit for a minute, just to think of his last Christmas with her, but it was raining now. He had to get home to Aunty Liza.

I'll have to really hurry, were his last thoughts before he was hit from behind and thrown down the slope.

Chapter Thirty-Three

From Twilight to Dawn

Philomena stood respectfully at the doorway peering anxiously at Zareen, who in turn was watching Bunny, hoping she would have something reassuring to say.

Then all three turned to Sherry as she walked into the room.

"Well?" asked both Zareen and Bunny in unison.

"No idea, no one knows. They rang the club but he's not there either."

"Something must have happened to him. Do you know which way he went?" asked Bunny.

"Must be the same route, surely?" asked Zareen, addressing the question to Philomena.

Disregarding Philo's weak nod, Bunny spoke up, breathless with excitement. "Considering the weather is absolutely foul and if he's had a fall, and don't forget he's also probably quite weak from all his depression or whatever it was you said he was going through, then we must look for him immediately otherwise he might die of hypothermia!" she finished dramatically, eagerly looking at everyone in the room, eyes wide and totally oblivious to

Zareen's frantic efforts in trying to get her to dilute her heart-breaking words before Philomena could absorb them.

"It'll be pitch dark in the next hour," said Sherry.

Bunny responded immediately. "Look, Dilip and the car are here, and you have Tiffany. We should really take both cars, so we find him as quickly as possible. Maybe best Dilip takes Tiff on a leash, and we go in your car, Sherry?"

"Yes, let's not waste time. It's best we start at both ends and meet in the middle," said Sherry.

Although they managed to reach Possession Lane in less than ten minutes, with Dilip taking the far end, it was already twilight when neither one's eyes nor headlights nor torches could help you see anything much beyond your nose, no matter how hard you tried. To top off the dismal situation they found themselves in, their spirits fell even further when they found the entire lane eerily silent and utterly deserted. Not a soul was in sight for them to check if anyone had seen Chinnaswamy earlier that evening.

They had barely a moment to put on anything warm when they rushed out of Buxey, so now found themselves shivering in the drizzle as they wandered about, frantically calling out Chinnaswamy's name as they struggled through the failing light. Their struggle, however, was short lived, as ten minutes into their search, Bunny received a call from Dilip to say that he had found Chinnaswamy, semi-conscious.

The morning light was welcome, despite it being barely there. Chinnaswamy gazed at it gratefully, as if it were an angelic light from heaven that had come down to bless him. He had returned to Buxey from a full twenty-four hour stay in the hospital. It had been an ordeal for them all, but Chinnaswamy, of course, had borne the brutal brunt of it. After he had been found, halfway down the bank, wedged, like a rag doll, between a thorny gorse bush and an old tree stump, he had been pulled up and rushed to hospital.

It was only at about midnight that he partially regained his senses. He had suffered multiple contusions from his right hip downwards, a fractured right ankle, torn ligaments on his left shoulder, and numerous cuts and bruises all over. For hours after being rescued, he could not speak. The fright of the terrible hit and run, the cold, the rain, and the pain of being stuck between what, he didn't know, for more than two hours, took their toll on the already fragile Chinnaswamy.

He could hardly remember his time in the hospital, nor for that matter could he recall what happened after being hit.

He stared at the light unblinking until his eyes slowly closed.

Chapter Thirty-Four

Forty-Eight Hours After the Accident

The Buttery, ten-fifteen a.m.

The silver cutlery twinkled from the numerous lights reflecting off it.

The fairly bright start to the day had quickly descended into a depressingly dark morning, quite the norm for the season, and the reason why, in anticipation, all the lights were switched on for the breakfast service.

The Buxey girls were halfway through breakfast.

"I think it's silly of us to have moved into the club for a whole week when we ought to be helping," whined Zareen as she dropped a massive dollop of bilberry jam onto her plate.

Sherry sighed as she watched the jam being spread thickly onto toast.

"Well, I think it's awfully selfish to stay at home when we can easily stay here for a couple of weeks and give poor Philo the time and space to nurse Chinnaswamy back to health. You know what she's like, Zee, always wanting to fuss unnecessarily for us when she has her own crisis going on. It's like a quirk she…"

She was interrupted by Daniel, asking if they wanted more coffee.

"Yes please, and stronger than usual if you can, thanks, Daniel."

Turning back to Zareen, she continued, although her tone was now hushed, and quite unnecessarily so, considering the room was empty.

"I hope you're thinking what I'm thinking, Zee."

"That Philo fusses extra when she's stressed?"

"Noooo, about C's accident!"

Getting nothing but a blank look in return, Sherry continued.

"It wasn't an accident. You have figured that much out, haven't you?"

"Oh my God, Sherry. What the heck is wrong with you? Are you going to now insist that this accident was something else quite sinister?"

"Sshhh… careful, Zee, Siva was killed in the next room. Who knows what is going on here? These walls and paintings have ears! And, yes, of course it wasn't an accident. I'd have thought you would have cottoned on to that at the get-go!"

Zareen's response was silence. In her opinion, it was just easier to not say anything than to have a tiresome argument.

Ignoring the silent treatment, Sherry lowered her voice even more, to a mere, albeit dramatic, whisper.

"Someone targeted him on purpose, and they wanted him dead. It's as plain as plain could be. I'm surprised at you," she finished uncharitably.

Although resolutely determined to keep her voice down too, Zareen's words came out in a hiss.

"Honestly, Sherry. No one knew Chinnaswamy was going to Mary's, so who'd have known where he was at that time to plan it all and manage to hit him with a car? Tell me who? No one!"

Her harsh words put an end to the one-sided conversation.

Room Number 6, noon

Sherry was alone. Zareen had popped back to Buxey to check if all was well with Philo and Chinnaswamy.

This was the first time she, and for that matter Zareen, had ever stayed at The Ooty Country Club, and they were thoroughly enjoying it. Their room was plush. The beds were properly set up with flat boards under extremely comfortable mattresses. They had a selection of therapeutic pillows to choose from, apart from standard pillows of various sizes and softnesses. For the life of them, they had no idea why they had never stayed at this beautiful club before, if for nothing other than a change of scenery.

She was sitting in an armchair, clutching a plump cushion to her chest as she stared out at the Camellia Lawn. She wondered if this is where all the trouble had started, on this very lawn amongst all the hoity-toity guests. Or maybe it was amongst the club staff?

Wherever it had started and whichever group of people it involved, she knew instinctively that someone still had unfinished business to deal with, that there would be another murder and if she did not make a momentous decision now, before Zareen returned to scupper her train of thought, it might be far too late.

She was at the crux of 'something', that much she knew, but had no idea what. Someone out there was a murderer, and that 'someone' could very probably be from their close circle.

The thought made her shudder. Her head hurt; she settled back in her chair and closed her eyes. Somewhere in her head lay the answer to it all but she couldn't put her finger on it. She thought back to the start of it all, to dear Mary's visit to tell her the AJ news; she remembered chatting to Ali at the club. Why was he so washed out and exhausted by AJ's death, considering people do die? She thought of when Phyllis called her to give the gory details of having been 'right there' when AJ was found, thrilled to bits she was. Then at the ball. How odd and nervy Violet seemed, and how Arun made that furtive exit before dinner was announced. Where did he go?

A wave of darkness overcame her. She thought of the bashed-in head of the poor dead boy, she thought of Chinnaswamy lying on the hospital bed, and of herself wondering if he would live or die. Yes, there was a killer out there who had to be stopped.

Willowbund Police Station, four p.m.

Sundar stared at her. Sherry's response was to nod her head vigorously. True to character, and after much rumination, Sherry had come up with a plan she felt was fool proof; at the very least, it was Zareen proof.

"You're sure about this?"

"Absolutely. We just have to give it a few more days, during which time I will slowly spread the word to all and sundry."

"I don't think we have anything to lose. If it actually happens, then we've caught the killer."

"Exactly. If nothing happens then we've lost nothing and are simply back to square one."

Chapter Thirty-Five

The Set-up

Three days later, Buxey Lodge, five p.m.

Are you sure he'll be all right, Sherry? Nothing will go wrong, will it? The thought of all this makes me nauseous, and dizzy, to boot," asked a nervous Zareen as she vigorously rubbed her icy arms.

Sherry was sitting opposite her, legs comfortably up on a footstool.

"Nope, absolutely not. These chaps know what they're doing. They've gone over the plan loads of times. They've assured me, and no one knows we're here. Not a soul except S.P. Raman. Not even your Mr Handsome Iqbal. Frankly, at the end of this, and if it turns out we were right, we'll have to be on a first name basis with those two, don't you think?"

"Oh, don't joke, Sherry, I'm absolutely terrified. I mean what happens if he, or she, or maybe even 'they', come into the house and attack us, or worse, turn the electricity off before coming for us?"

"Calm down. Nothing like that will happen. There are police everywhere on the grounds. There's a policeman inside the staff quarters as well because they want to prove the murderer intended to kill C. You see, there's every chance he can turn around and say he came just to visit Chinnaswamy, and then the whole plan will implode."

"Inside the quarters?"

"Yes, in the storeroom. The door that connects both rooms has been left open by a teeny crack, so as soon as he gets a message on his phone from the S.P. or whoever, he'll be on full alert."

"It sounds frightfully risky. What if he's scarred for life seeing the murderer or from being attacked?"

"It won't get to that, Zee. They'll make sure."

Noticing her tired tone, Zareen thought it best to keep her doubts to herself and plunged back into the topic of the set-up planned for tonight.

"I suppose he'll be safe enough considering that Chinnaswamy is more or less quite dead to the world from about seven-ish, thanks to his truckload of meds. He'll have no idea that anyone is even in the room. I think that was the smartest thing you thought of, Sherry. Telling everyone we're out of town this evening. What excuse did you give for us and Philo being out?"

"I simply said we were going to the Glenmorgan Estate to see our friends and that we were taking Philo as she has cousins there. And I did say the back door was going to be kept unlocked because the morning after our little 'idea' to help our Chinnaswamy out of his morbid fear of God knows what, we were also going to proudly tell him that the door was unlocked! The one thing we can rely on is the fact that as our friends visit us at Buxey so often, they know how to get around the house and the garden. I'm just hoping against hope, that is, if someone does turn up, that it's not anyone we know. It'll be mortifying."

She stopped at this point, saddened at the very thought of it.

"Sherry, if it is someone we know, then we have to jolly well thank our lucky stars they got caught! Be grateful if that's the case. Imagine hobnobbing for the next, I don't know how many years with someone who killed that poor boy and never knowing!"

Perking up at Zareen's attitude, Sherry continued, "And to be doubly sure they get all the evidence needed, I had them install the two CCTV cameras from our gate and garden. One is above Chinnaswamy's bed and the other one is just inside the back door, both very cleverly camouflaged. Not that we think he's going to take the time to look around. I hope you don't mind me not asking, but you were at Bunny's, and I didn't want anyone to hear you talking about CCTVs at Buxey."

"Yes, good thing you didn't call."

Buxey Lodge, six forty-five p.m.

All the lights in the house were turned off at six-thirty. Philo had been dispatched to Glenmorgan, having been told that her employers would keep an eye on her nephew.

Sherry and Zareen had moved a small sofa and positioned it right next to the door leading from the dining room to the kitchen. It was the closest they felt they could be to Chinnaswamy. They didn't want to sit at the table and risk the slightest sound by shifting around. They were told

215

they would get no alerts if someone actually turned up as there would be no time to let more than one person know, and their priority was their man positioned inside the staff quarters.

They settled down nervously, putting their mobiles on silent and deciding not to speak at all, just in case.

Buxey Lodge garden, nine p.m.

For once, Sundar ignored the fact that he was frozen stiff. After almost three hours of wondering if anything at all would transpire tonight, his eyes were now transfixed on what appeared to be the headlights of a car at the gate. His heart rate went up. He knew his people were watching too. It looked like the plan was going to work after all. After a moment, the headlights were turned off. Nothing more happened. Whoever it was, Sundar realised, was being very cautious.

After about five minutes, he could make out a car door opening very slowly and a shadow appearing out of it. It stood stock still for a moment, no doubt attempting to get a feel of the surroundings. Then a torch light came on. Focusing the light to the ground, the shadow started walking to the gate, opened it, and came into the garden. The shadow's silhouette now took proper shape and, dark as it was, could now be clearly seen as a person, awkwardly clutching something rather large and who seemed to know his, or her, way up to the house.

The footsteps picked up momentum as they progressed up the drive, no doubt gaining confidence with each step.

Reaching the top of the driveway, and now being quite close to the house, the figure stopped, seemingly to get their bearings, then purposefully walked right past the front door to the end of the house and then made a sharp left turn.

Whoever this person was, they knew exactly where the staff quarters were.

Sundar was thankful that he had done numerous dry runs on how many seconds it would take a perpetrator to attack Chinnaswamy once they were inside. He knew for sure that there would be no loitering. The deed would be done swiftly, as a quick exit was imperative for his safety.

From the CCTV app on his phone, he could see the dark figure enter through the back door, once again standing still for a few moments. Sundar knew the alert had been sent to their man positioned inside. He could now see that it was a pillow that had been carried into the house.

He didn't blink once as he stared at his phone. It was just a matter of seconds now... and... CAUGHT!

Chapter Thirty-Six

Explanations and Exclamations

"You're joking?"

"No, I'm not, darling."

"Like a scene from a real movie?"

"Seems so, yes, and all of you are invited."

Leo couldn't believe his ears. Invited to hear the full story of who killed the club boy and why it happened!

"Dad's coming?"

"Yes, he's getting back this afternoon. Absolutely everyone has been asked."

"But why don't we know who it is? Seeing as he was caught two nights ago!" Leo asked, miffed.

"Patience, my boy, the police have had to do an awful lot of questioning, so Sherry said."

"What time?"

"It's at six, drinks followed by dinner."

"Must be a lot of people coming, seeing as we're six already."

"I'm sure. Sherry said there'd be quite a crowd, and that includes your friend, Sam, who was with you in the dining room so remember to bring him, too."

The driveway up to Buxey Lodge was brightly lit which was a great help to the cars battling the thick mist as they drove up.

The Ponnappas fetched up in two starkly different cars. Arriving first was Leo, driving a muddy Land Rover with his sisters and Sam. They were followed moments later by his parents in a mud free, gleaming silver Rolls.

They entered a loud and crowded sitting room. Everyone was talking at the top of their voice. Dimple saw Daniel and Bartholomew huddled in a corner, nervous but obviously thrilled at the extraordinary invitation they received.

She noticed they were in their Sunday best and startled by the appearance of a drinks tray offered to them, but they were too shy to pick up a glass. She saw Liza wheeling Chinnaswamy in, the poor fellow was still in a wheelchair of course. He was settled in next to his club chums.

Although it seemed to her that every person she knew, even those merely by sight, was here, people were still streaming in. It was the two senior police officers now, looking rather pleased with themselves. She arched a perfect eyebrow as she noted Miki, trust him to make a beeline for them with a wide smile, hurriedly shooing a waiter towards them. Aaaaah well, typical Miki, but best to keep on the right side of the police, she concluded.

The atmosphere in the room was light-hearted with an air of celebration. A gathering of good friends in a warm, beautiful house, trays of drinks being served up, and three varieties of hot curry puffs was just what the doctor had ordered to lift their spirits from the chill and gloom outside. Dimple looked around earnestly. She knew that someone would be absent from the guest list tonight, but she just couldn't figure out who the missing person was. There were just too many people milling about, then of course, there may still be people yet to arrive. Where was Bunny, she wondered, thinking fondly of her like-minded friend from her home country. She smiled as she imagined clutching both Miki and Bunny's arms in high excitement as they were finally given the name of the murderer.

Goose pimples ran up her arms. This was a strange setting, right out of a movie. She rubbed her arms vigorously as her eyes continued to search for Bunny.

Her thoughts were interrupted by a glass being clinked so vigorously with a canapé fork that she winced. The culprit was Johnny Chacko.

The Brigadier's formidable figure, walrus moustache, and glass clinking was all that was needed to instantly stop the cacophony in the room.

"My friends, I know you're all anxiously waiting to hear the full story behind the despicable murder in the club. Our Sherry, having been brilliantly quick on the uptake from the very beginning, will now explain."

All eyes turned to Sherry, standing near the Brigadier. She gave them all a wide, albeit apprehensive grin, before starting her story.

"Hi all! I'm so glad that each one of you accepted this very last-minute invite! I'm going to try my best to explain what happened and I'm warning you that it's turned out to be a much longer story than we all thought! So, here goes... as I always suspected, this shocking chapter in our lives started at the President's Tea party, back in May, when a casual chat between two people took place. That chat was the reason two people, yes, two people, were killed and an attempted murder was made on another, not once, but twice."

Although it wasn't in her nature, Sherry paused for effect. No one had any idea that more than one death would be spoken of tonight. Perplexed eyes stared back at her, quickly followed by exclamations of disbelief but before questions were hurled at her, she continued.

"The first murder, originally deemed a natural death, and we can't blame anyone for deducing it as anything but …" she faltered for a second before continuing, studiously avoiding catching Dr Danny's eye at this point, "… was that of AJ Panniker, a man some of us knew, and many of us did not. The second savage murder was of the young club boy, Siva, whom, sadly, none of us save the club staff, knew at all.

"And then we have the story of a mentally challenged youngster. A youngster who saw something, seemingly of no significance, on the night of the first murder and then saw it again days later, except that on this second occasion, the object in question meant something momentous to him. That youngster is Chinnaswamy, who as you all know, is our maid's nephew and works at the club, and who has an underdeveloped brain. He cannot 'catch' all his thoughts when he wants to or even when he is asked to. On many occasions, it may never return but sometimes it does. And that is what the killer simply could not risk.

"Tragically, the killer was in the same room when he saw the item the second time around and understood with great clarity that the expression on the young man's face meant, not only that he knew that AJ Panniker had been

221

killed at the country club, but also how it was done... and by whom. The killing of Siva was totally unplanned. The murderer found opportunity, by chance, standing in an empty dining room with Siva and, seizing the chance, picked up the poker and smashed it down on his head. The poor, skinny boy collapsed immediately."

Sherry stopped to take a sip of her drink and catch her breath. She felt exhilarated, but at the same time sad at the news she was about to reveal. The entire room stood patiently, having been stunned into silence by just the first few minutes of Sherry's speech. Putting her glass down, she continued.

"I'll now go back to the beginning. To the President's Tea, the day AJ Panniker decided to make his grand entrance into Ooty high society.

"AJ was a mean-spirited man. Given the chance, he would grab every opportunity to upset the apple cart, and it was his attempt at upsetting one such apple cart on that beautiful sunny day in May that caused his untimely death.

"AJ cosied up to Brigadier Chacko at the garden party, and for no apparent reason, started talking to him about the upcoming changes to the club committee, changes he had heard about through the club grapevine as soon as he had checked in, barely two days earlier. He had the audacity to criticise their decision to appoint a female member, alluding that it would not bode well for the club in the long run. Sadly for AJ, the female member in question was in earshot of the conversation and decided to take matters into her own hands.

"Mary interrupted the two men and Brigadier Chacko, relieved to be relieved of the obnoxious AJ, gratefully picked up a chat with Mary.

"No one watching the club president having an animated chat with his old friend Mary Mendoza in that beautifully perfect setting would have any idea that behind her twinkling eyes, the wheels in her head were turning violently. She knew she had to get rid of AJ, she knew if he hung around, even for a few days more, he may well set the seed of doubt in the minds of the committee members."

At this point Sherry was forced to stop. Everyone had started talking. This was a double whammy. The AJ Panniker many had heard of, if not met, during his brief stay in town had been murdered, and murdered by their darling Mary, of all people. Some gasped at the unbelievable thought of Mary Mendoza, someone from their own circle for God's sake, killing AJ Panniker. Some turned their heads as they searched around the room, so sure where they that they had seen Mary... somewhere... but... where? ... and had they actually seen her?

"Mary? Not capable, surely..." said Arun loudly but trailed off after a withering look from Violet.

"So, the Johnny-come-lately met our Johnny!" yelled out Geoffrey, causing laughter around the room.

Sherry took this opportunity to have another sip of her Bloody Mary, turning around to catch Zareen's eye, she gave her a wistful smile. It was out. Their trusted old friend Mary had, all along, been the 'mad murderer about town'!

Brigadier Chacko started clinking a glass again, except now it sounded more like a frantic clanging. Silence was restored.

"How did she do it, Sherry?" shouted out a highly animated Phyllis with Geoffrey beside her, nodding energetically.

"Well, that's the part I'm trying to get to, darling! Mary, as you all know is, was, gosh I don't know what tense to use! Anyway, I'm going to say 'was'! Mary was a very old member of the club. She knew the club, literally inside out, the many corridors and where they led, and more importantly, in this case, the doors. She knew, probably better than some club employees, which door could take her where and how quickly. Seeing Mary standing in a corridor that a guest normally would not use was nothing unusual for the staff.

"The night AJ was murdered, Mary, as usual, went to the club for dinner, with every intention of killing AJ.

"The club staff were exhausted after the President's Tea. All they wanted was for the evening to be over and to get to bed.

"Mary had taken poison with her, knowing exactly how she would administer it. Having been at the club the previous two evenings for dinner, she knew that AJ had had his dinner served in his room on both evenings. It was likely that on that fateful night, he would once again order room service.

"She also knew that the room service timing for dinner was always between eight and eight forty-five. Not earlier, not later. That was no problem for Mary, after all she was at the club almost all nights from about seven-fifteen to about eight-thirty. No one would notice if she lingered another fifteen minutes longer that night if she needed to.

"Mary sat at her usual table for dinner. At precisely seven fifty-five, in the middle of her meal, she visited the Ladies' powder room. She could not afford to lose the very small window between a trolley being loaded in the utility corridor and when it would be wheeled out. For all she knew, AJ may well have ordered his dinner for eight. If that was the case, she had to be there at precisely the right time. She also knew that she may have to make subsequent trips to the corridor if his dinner had been ordered for later.

"Once inside the Ladies' powder room, she went straight to the back door that leads into the utility corridor. Many of you may not know that this passage is deemed the reason why the club machinery works so well. It was constructed after the main building came up and is an extension along the back wall of the building that runs along its full length. It is a single, long corridor with a door at either end and multiple doors along one side. One of the end doors, at the back end near the kitchen, is for suppliers to enter directly from outside, and the door opposite it leads into the main clubhouse giving the staff a shortcut to the guest rooms. Then there are four doors along the side of the corridor, adjacent to the original clubhouse wall. One leads into the kitchen, the next door leads into the dining room, then there is a door to each of the Gents and Ladies, for the cleaning staff to enter. Mary walked boldly out of the back door of the Ladies. It hardly took her twenty steps to reach the end of the passage, near the kitchen door. Three trolleys had been laid out and would be wheeled to the respective guest rooms. Luck was on her side. One of the trolleys had his room number on its card. She knew which room he was staying in as she had made it a point to find out at the garden party.

"AJ had only ordered soup. The empty mini soup tureen was on the trolley. It would be filled with piping hot soup at the very last minute, just before the trolley was being wheeled out. An empty soup bowl was duly laid upside down on its underlay plate, also on the trolley. She deftly lifted the tureen lid, sprinkled the poison powder into the empty dish, replaced the lid, and was back inside the Ladies' powder room in not more than fifteen seconds.

"But there was a hitch. She was seen by Chinnaswamy who was hauling in bag after bag of firewood through the supplier's entrance door.

"He saw her, she saw him. However, neither of them thought anything of it. Miss Mary Ma'm, as Chinnaswamy referred to her, was a fixture at the club, and don't forget, the employer of his beloved Aunty Liza. Seeing her in the middle of the utility passage meant nothing to him. He went about his business, and she returned to her meal having done the deed.

"However, many evenings later, Chinnaswamy was visiting his Aunt Liza in Mary's home. In actual fact, Zareen and I were also there later that evening.

"Just before we arrived at Nun's Cross, Chinnaswamy arrived to meet his aunt. His friend, Siva, had also tagged along. It was during their visit that evening when an unfortunate event occurred. While Liza was serving her nephew and his friend a cup of tea, Mary arrived in the kitchen to talk about putting out rat poison for the rats in the garden. During the conversation, Liza opened a cupboard to check the stock of poison. The boys, with nothing else to do, watched the interaction between the ladies. There was one tin left and Liza said there wasn't much in it. Mary picked up the tin to check the contents and, whilst doing so, an image popped up in Chinnaswamy's head, an image of Mary standing in the utility corridor of the club, on the night of AJ's death, clutching the same tiny red tin in her hand.

"To the boy's very bad luck, Mary had seen the sudden look of utter enlightenment on Chinnaswamy's face, and she knew exactly what it meant! It meant two things: firstly, that Chinnaswamy had recognised the tin as the same one she was clutching as she walked towards the dinner trolleys that night; and secondly, he knew what she had done and so, how AJ Panniker died.

"Mary, as we have now learned, has a mind of steel. Her reaction was to merely smile sweetly at Chinnaswamy and return to her sitting room. She knew what she had to do but there was no hurry; Chinnaswamy, likely as not, would forget his realisation practically instantaneously, but the memory would come back one day, this she knew for sure.

"Now we fast track to the Equestrian Ball. A week before the ball, Mary had made it clear to all of us that she had no intention of staying right through to dinner, but having seen the splendid dinner spread, for this event in the past, she decided to peep in for a 'look see' before she left for the evening. From experience, she knew the dining room doors would be bolted no later than eight-fifteen. It was now eight twenty-five, so she went to the Ladies, and as she did before, exited through the back door and into the corridor. She walked the few steps to the dining room door. She turned the handle, it was unlocked, the door opened, and she walked in. She thought nothing of it, for her it was the norm to be prowling around the club, unexpectedly popping up at the oddest nooks and crannies. In her mind, she envisaged herself to be looked upon by the club staff as, 'She, the startlingly unpredictable, but much respected, One'.

"So, there was Mary, taking in the sight of tables beautifully laid out with canapés, overflowing platters intertwined with numerous vases of flowers, when she sensed someone behind her.

"Unperturbed, she turned to see who it was. Chinnaswamy! She could scarcely believe her extraordinary luck. She realised this was her perfect opportunity. No one would come in. She could clearly hear Ali's voice in the kitchen, still giving his brief.

"She walked up behind him as he was bending over the blazing fire, immersed in trying to put it out without making too much of a mess. Don't forget, it was roaring. He couldn't hear her quiet steps behind him. Poor chap probably didn't even notice her when she walked in. Mary was wearing a sari. Quickly grabbing a part of her sari, as a pseudo glove, she picked up the heavy poker and smashed it down on his head. He fell immediately. She checked the pulse on his neck. He had died with that one blow. In all her excitement of having so quickly achieved her plan to kill Chinnaswamy, she had not noticed it was Siva. Angry with the boy for having 'caught her out' the other day, she maliciously brought down the poker onto his head three more times. So possessed was she that she thought nothing of the risk she was taking with the extra time she spent smashing his head.

"She then dropped the poker, left the dining room in the same way that she had entered, and went to the back door of the Ladies' powder room. She remained standing outside. At this point she had to be very careful. She knew there may be someone inside the Ladies, she could not risk being seen entering through the back door. She waited patiently for that critical moment when all was silent inside, she then quickly entered and walked straight out through the main door and back into the club hall, where she immediately started her goodbyes for the evening!

"As we all know now, Mary left the ball a few minutes after the murder, thoroughly delighted with herself."

At this point a loud murmur started up amongst the audience; many of them turned towards the small 'club group', tut tutting at the lucky escape the injured youngster had. In turn, Chinnaswamy, the man of the moment, grinned at all the sympathetic faces, relishing the sudden attention.

Sherry battled on, raising her voice to regain attention. "The following day, she got the shock of her life when she heard from her maid that the murder victim was not Chinnaswamy, but Siva, Chinnaswamy's best friend. She now had to lay out a concrete plan to make sure the next attempt was fool proof.

"When Chinnaswamy heard the news, he was devastated, going into shock and having a minor breakdown. He couldn't explain his worry, sadness, fear, or whatever it was, to anyone, because he couldn't understand it nor pin down what the issue was. The one thing he did know was that he was terrified of going to his Aunty Liza's, at The Hermitage. We all put it down to the fact that the property's close proximity to the club was what he feared most. Then we all started hearing a rumour, started by Mary, that he was in fact scared of Francis. We now know that in his subconscious mind, he knew Mary was behind Siva's murder, but again, it was all a muddle in his head. The realisation was there somewhere, floating about in his mind, but never appearing with full clarity.

"With his breakdown causing him to stay put here in Buxey, Mary now had to plan very, very carefully. She remained calm, however, supremely confident in her knowledge that the mental breakdown he was suffering simply gave her more time. She also knew that until he came out of our compound, there was no chance she could deal with the 'problem'!

"She bided her time; let him stay put for a bit, she decided. She took advantage of Liza, speaking to her often about the boy. Mary gave her confidence that all would be well eventually and when she thought the time was right, she slowly started coaxing Liza into visiting her nephew. She advised her to remain her cheerful self, bake his favourite cookies, and hang out with Philomena, create a normal environment, all in the knowledge that Chinnaswamy, being closer to Liza than Philomena, could well be persuaded by Liza to visit her at The Hermitage. The visit, if it happened, is when she would strike.

"All her life, Mary was an observer. She knew the oddest details about those around her. In this case, she knew that if Liza managed to get him to visit, he would use the route he had used since his mother died, which was to walk to The Hermitage through Possession Lane. I'm sure some of you may not even know of this lane, it's a quiet little path, just off the centre of town and those who know of it, use it often as a convenient shortcut to get about.

"She also had the bad weather on her side. We all know that we Ooty-ites like to be indoors by the time evening falls during the monsoon. There would be fewer people, more likely none at all, on the lane.

"She advised Liza to ask him to arrive in the evening, telling her that if he said yes to arriving between six and six-thirty, then it meant he was on the clear road to recovery, meaning if he was happy to get out and about in the evening, it was a sure sign that he was getting back to normal. So, Liza did as she was told and Chinnaswamy agreed. Actually, Mary had been right; the normal, happy, chatty evening spent in our kitchen the night Liza visited did perk him up enormously.

"The day she heard Chinnaswamy had agreed to come, she acted on her plan. She asked Francis to go in his car to Possession Lane to pick up plants from a nursery. Her excuse was that her driver was on leave and her eyes were no good in the fog. She even gave him the time to pick up the plants. Francis was going to be the fall guy.

"Knowing that Francis would be on Possession Lane at about four that afternoon, and knowing that Chinnaswamy would be passing by, at the earliest, around five-thirty, a hit and run could be blamed on Francis. Her accusation would be based on her theory, which was that Francis could have parked his car in one of the many nooks overgrown with shrubs, waiting for the boy to arrive. After all, she and Liza had told him they had managed to get Chinnaswamy to come over. Mary could claim that she even told Francis that he was likely to walk over through the lane…"

231

Sherry's voice was now totally drowned out. Loud voices started asking Francis all sorts of questions. "Did you have any idea, Francis?" shouted out Geoffrey, whose voice was the loudest. But before 'the very pleased with himself Francis' could bellow out a reply, Johnny Chako started clinking glasses again, successfully silencing the room. A grateful, albeit slightly frazzled, Sherry was now able to continue.

"So, as I was saying, Mary saw Francis arriving back at about four-thirty. She had already told him she would pick up the plants from him the following day because it would be cold and wet that evening. She had given Liza the evening off, telling her to cook a nice dinner for her nephew.

"She slipped out at just after five. Got into her car, confident no one would notice, and drove to Possession Lane. She parked the car behind a large bush making sure the car was partially hidden by it. She waited patiently until our poor Chinnaswamy sauntered by. He walked right past her car, as she expected. She waited a good three to four minutes after he passed her, then slowly started up her car and drove behind him. He didn't suspect anything was amiss. She hit him from behind and drove off. She thought she had finally succeeded, but she hadn't, thanks to her poor eyesight. That part was true. She really couldn't see that well in the fog and mist, and especially not in that poor evening light. She only managed to hit him on his right side, damaging his hip. He fell off the road and down the slope. The impact of the fall was almost as bad as being hit by the car, but he lived.

"That evening, Mary once again got the fright of her life when she heard from Liza that the missing Chinnaswamy was found alive and had been rushed to the hospital. She was in fact beside herself with her dismal failure; the effort that had gone into the planning of the hit and run had drained her, she had also been on tenterhooks for days before the attempt, tense with the worry of whether or not Chinnaswamy could actually be coaxed out of the house and if yes, would he, indeed, take that all-important route through Possession Lane.

"In the days that followed Chinnaswamy's slow recovery, she was clueless on how to plan her next move. There was no way she could get access to him now, firmly ensconced as he was, in the staff quarters in Buxey.

"And then, barely a week after her attempt to kill him, she got her big break. She heard, from **us** no less, as did so many of our friends and acquaintances; in fact we told every passer-by in the hope that word would filter down to absolutely everyone in town, that we had a big plan in mind, and it was all because we were terribly worried about Chinnaswamy's mental health. To be honest, this sort of exercise could only work in a tiny town like ours, where everyone is connected, in some way, at least. We told everyone that we feared he would regress even further back than he had before because of the accident and his painful injuries. We told everyone that our plan was to give him a huge shot of self-confidence, by going off for an overnight stay at the Glenmorgan Estate with our friends, who own the plantation, and that Philomena would be coming with us as well. We said that as we didn't want to alarm him, we were going to tell him that only Philo was going off and that

Zee and I were at home in case he needed something. We made it plain to all that we were very confident that he would be fine because we knew for a fact that his evening medication knocked him out completely. He wouldn't stir till dawn. The next day, we would tell him that not only were all three of us out of the house the entire night but that the kitchen door was unlocked! The plan was that the 'experience' of having managed to be alone overnight would give him the badly needed confidence to get on with things on his own and not be such a 'fraidy cat'!

"Our real plan, of course, was to get the message out to whomever the guilty party was, that the house would be completely deserted that night, except for the still-invalid Chinnaswamy. If the murderer was someone familiar with Buxey Lodge, then he would know that Chinnaswamy would be in the staff quarters. It was a gamble, though, as we had no idea who the murderer was; he, or she as it turned out in this case, could have been a washer upper in the club, which meant they would have no idea about the house and where he would be in it! But we simply had to take the plunge. We couldn't risk another death, or as is quite often the case, a situation where the killings suddenly stop for no apparent reason, leaving us all in the dark, wondering for years down the line, when every time we looked at someone, if they were 'the club killer'. Hang on for a minute, all. I need a sip of my drink!"

Sherry plonked herself down for a badly needed gulp of her drink. She also needed a moment to collect her thoughts and rest her voice. The room immediately erupted in chatter. Everyone was talking at the very top of their voices. Many made a beeline for Francis, making sympathetic noises. Francis in turn, twirling his glass of Scotch, his lanky figure leaning against the mantelpiece, regaled his sympathisers with his long-held instincts about Mary. He had always known something was 'off' with her.

Ali, who was standing a short distance away from his staff, started nudging himself closer to their corner. Sympathy and camaraderie were, after all, basic human instincts.

"Sherry, so what happened next?" yelled out Geoffrey.

"Well, after having hatched the plan, we needed to go to the police..."

She was cut short by Zareen butting in.

"It wasn't a case of 'we', it was Sherry's idea!" she finished, with a knowing grin.

"Okay, okay, it was I who went to see S.P. Raman..." Pausing, she turned to give him a smile in acknowledgement, "... and told him my plan. Thankfully he agreed straightaway and, of course, he and D.S.P. Iqbal did all the intricate planning to make sure if anyone turned up, that they would be caught red-handed. They placed policemen all over the garden, hidden behind bushes and, most importantly, they managed to get one of them into the storeroom next to Chinnaswamy's room after he fell asleep.

"Then all we had to do was to sit in complete darkness and wait, hoping against hope the murderer had heard that the house was empty and would risk another attempt. We waited and waited. It seemed like half the night had passed, but it was just around nine that a car turned up at our gate and the driver emerged.

"As you all now know, that driver was Mary. She made her way straight to the maid's accommodation and walked in with a pillow, yes a pillow, of all things, was her chosen weapon. She had planned to suffocate Chinnaswamy with it and was caught just as she was about to bring the pillow down over his face."

Sherry stopped abruptly. There was nothing more to say. She turned to speak to Zareen, but her words were drowned by the cacophony that engulfed the room. She gazed across the spacious sitting room, realising that it had never held so many people from so many walks of life at one time. With a twinge, she wondered if she would ever again be involved in something as serious as these murders; could she be entering another phase of her life?... after all, I'm getting on rather well with the police now... she said to herself.

"We'll need a round of stiff drinks now, Sherry," shouted Geoffrey.

"Yea sure, Geoff. The Screwallahs and Pearl have a huge stash in the kitchen."

The End

Acknowledgements

The first person we must acknowledge is an acquaintance who cannot be named! 'He', who strutted into our home, and whose grandiloquent behaviour raised many an eyebrow, was the unwitting inspiration for us to sit down, with some urgency, and say, 'heck, we **have** to write a story with him in it'. So, in the setting of an idyllic wildlife sanctuary, a plot was devised amongst the three of us, which ended up on the back burner until COVID-19 lockdowns afforded us the time to sit and write 'Blood, With A Drop of Sherry'.

The second person we have to thank profusely is Shova Loh, who was the publishing manager at Times Editions, Singapore, when we first met in Frankfurt. An old friend and brilliant colleague to work with, Shova very kindly read the first portion of 'Blood' and gave us a resounding thumbs up as well as some jolly good pointers. Thank you, Shova!

Alongside Shova, Jennifer Grubb, a true blue Nilgiri-ite, whose invaluable inputs and encouragement on the early pages of the book were invaluable. Thank you so much, dear Jen.

When the first draft was ready, it was Mrs. Patricia Finlay who topped our list for an opinion. A dear family friend, from our years growing up in beautiful Hong Kong. Many thanks and so very many hugs, Mrs. Finlay, for the time you devoted to the very rough draft we sent you!

A very special thanks to Cydney O'Sullivan, a childhood friend and founder of the successful publishing company, Celebrity Publishers. Thank you, Cyd, for the invaluable points you brought up with the early draft you so diligently went through.

An enormous thank you to Claire Chao, who was and is a constant support with invaluable insights and information. A huge hug to Donna Miller, who got me in touch with Claire after so many years.

And to dear Louise Luck, thank you so much for all your kindness, and to think the last time we met, we were just kids... Louise, Donna, Claire, Cyd and the Finlay family, we shared those magnificent years together in Hong Kong, and none of us will ever forget them.

Grateful thanks to our close friends, the Vaderas, who graciously consented to our use of their breathtaking estate and delicious tea throughout the writing of the book, and to Anushree Mathias for her ever present 'can-do will-do' persona.

Sincere thanks to Rozario, Nandithaa and Isha for their patience and precious time right through the writing of this book.

Thank you **all**!